DIBS

MELISSA SENGER

Melissa Senger

Title: Dibs

Author: Melissa Senger

Cover: Vanilla Lily Designs

 Formatted with Vellum

❧ 1 ❧

ASPYN

I'm watching the clock the second it strikes midnight, anger ratcheting up with every second that passes.

Sean is late again, and his dumb ass left his Kindle charging on the counter, revealing a string of explicit messages with someone named "Nurse Q."

It's not the first time he's cheated, but it's the first time I have this kind of evidence. Hell, I'm not even sure the first time he cheated, years ago, was the first indiscretion. Sean never copped to it, leaving me with my suspicions and no solid answers.

Instead, he gaslit me into thinking I was crazy, and how I could "ever dare" accuse him of such a terrible thing.

Okay, maybe I'm the dumb ass.

I'm standing here in my satin robe, rereading the chain of messages that are inappropriate at best, then pacing the tile of the kitchen. It's beyond late.

What am I doing waiting up for this asshole?

Naturally, I swing open the freezer and dig in it for a forbidden Fudge Pop I'd hidden in a bag of peas. Sean was always more worried about my "womanly figure" than I was,

1

and any sweet snacks I bought at the store I had to consume in the car before the drive home, or hide in the bedroom in places he wouldn't expect.

What an asshole.

The more I think about his control over my food choices, the redder my face gets, and the more pissed off I become. As I devour the Fudge Pop, my hands shake. My left eye twitches in annoyance, and then the right one joins in, like they've coordinated this pleasureless dance of aggravation.

I swipe my hand over my eye and hold the eyelid down tightly, my lips a thin line as I shove them together and refuse to let them tremble.

I will not let this make me cry.

Fuck.

I glance at the clock—12:12 a.m.

Tomorrow is the big day. Not mine, thank gods, but Sean's sister Tara is finally marrying her long-time boyfriend. They've been together for nine years, and I've been with her idiot brother for almost ten. She is marrying an outstanding surgical technician. Sean had introduced her to from his work, and he's a man who comes home at a reasonable hour, respects her, and never sexts other women.

Tara asked me a long time ago to be a bridesmaid because we're practically family, and I've been helping her plan the perfect early-September wedding, without a ring on my own finger, for the past year.

Sean's Kindle vibrates beside me on the counter.

The last message Sean sent was telling Nurse Q that she's sexy and luscious, going on to ask if she was wet and ready for him. I read her response urging him to hurry home, wrinkling my nose and scrunching up my face in disgust.

Hands still shaking, I take a quick picture of the exchange, knowing Sean can't gaslight his way out of this now. Not that he wouldn't try. He's a skilled narcissist. I've learned that from watching so many TikTok videos, and I beat myself up every day for not realizing sooner.

Can I give myself permission to leave him now?

Is his crime finally bad enough to give up on nearly ten years of my youth and say, "Fuck it?"

Fuck this.

I toss Sean's Kindle into the bedroom I share with him and make up the pull-out sofa for him, moving his phone charger from the bedroom to the living room.

I hang his best tux in the hall closet along with the special tie he'll be wearing as the Best Man, and set his shiny alligator leather shoes in there, too.

Then, I tear a piece of paper out of a notebook and, fuming, I write a note.

I hope you had a lovely time with Nurse Q tonight. I'm glad she's so luscious, sexy, and endlessly wet for your 'giant' (PSA: really quite average) cock. Nothing you can say will excuse your behavior. I am DONE. We're done. I've waited ten years for a ring that never came, while you've been busy getting off with random nurses. Any self-respecting woman would leave you, so that's what I'm doing.

Tomorrow, we will arrive separately at Tara's wedding, be on our best behavior, and celebrate her nuptials. We will not dance together. You won't touch me. I will bite you. We won't tell anyone we broke up, because it's Tara's day. After that, I'll come home. You'll find somewhere else to go for the 30 days it will take me to find another place to live. If you fight me on this, I'll make you legally evict me, which takes months, and I will make sure the entire hospital knows you're a cheating bastard. Your clothes are in the coat closet.

When I release my death grip on the expensive pen Sean's boss had given him for Christmas last year, I let out a sigh of relief—ten years with this man have been too many. I've cried so many tears in those years that I'm finding none tonight. Anger, though—hell, I have that in spades.

I pop a sleeping pill and send Sean's best friend, Deacon Ambrose, a text. He's become more like my best friend over the years, given Sean's crazy hours as an emergency room physician. I wonder briefly who will get Deacon in the breakup as I text him.

ME:

> Sean cheated again. This time it's really over. Don't make a big deal of it tomorrow. We don't want anyone to know yet. Just let me get through the wedding before you give me one of those bear hugs that will make me cry.

I SEND THE MESSAGE, THANK THE MEDICINE FOR KICKING IN so fast, and fall into a blessed, deep sleep.

2

ASPYN

My emerald-green strapless dress, with a sweetheart neckline, clings to my curves perfectly. I sit patiently in the bridal suite, waiting for the make-up artist Tara hired to get around to me. I'm on my fourth mimosa in two hours, and my second plate is filled with fruit and croissants.

"You're strangely quiet," my friend and fellow bridesmaid, Wendy, says, nudging me as she sits beside me on the sofa.

"Just taking it all in. It's been such a wonderful morning, and I'm excited today is finally here." I manage a convincing smile that says, "Hey, I'm chill, I'm definitely not panic drinking, and my heart is certainly not in pieces within my chest." At least, that's what I hope my smile says.

Sean will get Tara in the breakup. Our days of couples' travel and co-hosting huge parties will be over, and everything I have grown accustomed to is going to change entirely. *That* thought nearly brings tears to my eyes, but I disguise it by adding, "And what a beautiful bride you are, Tara. You've never looked more beautiful!"

Her cream-colored, poofy princess dress is exactly what

she's always dreamed of, and her gorgeous red hair is styled in a half-updo, pinned with silver combs featuring tiny pearls to match her necklace. The rest of her hair hangs freely down her back. She is stunning, and, by far, one of the kindest people I've ever met. How she and Sean were raised by the same parents in the same home and turned out as complete opposites is beyond my understanding. But, I try not to dwell.

"Don't make me cry, Aspyn!" Tara scolds me with a fake glare and a wink. "But thank you. I think I've nailed the princess look, and this make-up is perfect! Get over here, sis, it's your turn. Blink those tears away."

I pull myself together and take Tara's place in the make-up chair in front of a mirror lit by a dozen bright bulbs. Sitting still while Tara's friend creates a neutral color palette on my face is a challenge because I'm feeling particularly twitchy. Finally, Amber adds a little pink sparkly eyeshadow and a pretty mauve lipstick.

Glancing in the mirror, I look like a pin-up model—minus the classic red lip—that's how excellent Amber is at her job.

The dress perfectly matches my tattoo sleeve, which features a forest of dark green and brown evergreen trees under a backdrop of purple and green swirling Northern Lights, the moon, and the constellation Sagittarius, my star sign.

Tara's hands fall to my shoulders as she stands behind me, smiling at me in the mirror. Our eyes connect, and I beg my top lip not to tremble. *Do not lose it. Now isn't the time!*

"You look incredible, Sis."

It melts the smile right off my face. We will never be family. Never be sisters-in-law.

Not now.

"Hey, where did you just go?"

"Sorry." I wince. "Your brother and I aren't in the best place right now."

My voice lowers to a whisper, not wanting to draw attention from the other women. This is Tara's day. Soon enough, she will know everything, and I want to be the one to tell her after she returns from the honeymoon. God only knows what terrible slant Sean will put on it. My heart shatters at the thought of more lies from my narcissist ex.

"I thought you were trying to have a baby?" Tara's eyes narrow as she stares back at me, tilting her head to the side.

"We were not actively trying not to. He thought if he could give me a baby, I would stop asking for a ring, I guess." I frown for a second before shrugging. "I'm okay. Let's focus on you, babe. It's your wedding day!"

"Okay, but as soon as we get home from the honeymoon, it's you, me, and a gallon of ice cream and bad reality TV. Got it?"

Supplying Tara with a reluctant smile, I wonder if that date will ever happen.

A knock sounds at the door.

When I see Deacon standing there, tears rush to my eyes and my hands start to tremble. He has this unique ability...when he looks at me, I feel as though he's looking through me, down to the ooey-gooey center I don't let anyone see. Viewing the deepest and most vulnerable parts of me that I prefer to hide. And all I know is, now is not the time for that.

"You look stunning." Deacon takes my hand, pulls me through the doorway, and lets the bridal suite door shut behind me. "But I can tell you're barely holding on. I read your text this morning. How are you doing?" His voice is full of empathy.

"Pretty badly." I stare up into his clear blue eyes and gulp three times hard to keep a sob from bursting from me. "Tara knows that her brother and I are having problems, but she doesn't know the extent. Or that it's over."

"Sean's acting like it's not over downstairs. He's discussing how you two are trying to get pregnant. Of course, everyone's asking when he will marry you and make an honest woman out of you." Deacon rolls his eyes and sighs.

"That man knows nothing about honesty." My hands shake as Deacon takes them into his much-bigger hands and squeezes. "I fucking hate him so much right now."

"I'd be lying if I said I wasn't disgusted too. We've been friends since high school, but he's clearly the guilty party here." Deacon's gaze is empathetic.

"Look, Deac."

"Don't 'look, Deac,' me," he interrupts. "I know what you're going to say, but if you insist...go for it."

"I don't want to get between you two. But I get it if you have to take his side in this one, since you've known Sean the longest." My voice is full of nerves I don't feel, and then I run out of words.

It's an outright lie.

In that moment, I might die if Deacon stands up for Sean after all the ways he's hurt and gaslit me over the last decade. Deacon is too good a person. Too generous, compassionate, and sweet to side with a guy like Sean. A slimeball. They couldn't be more different if they tried, despite being long-time friends. Sean hadn't always been terrible, though, had he? He was a lot of fun despite being pre-med in college, and he was charming as hell. People loved him wherever he went, and he liked having me, the beauty, on his arm.

His hand cups my face as I look at the floor, the hexagonal pattern on the rug dancing as my eyes blur. "You're not going to get rid of me that easily. Besides, Sean is a shitty friend nine times out of ten, and if he makes me choose, I will choose the better human being. And if you don't immediately know who that is, I don't know what to tell ya." His lips quirk up around the edges.

Our eyes meet, and another vulnerable feeling passes

through me again, sending a shiver down my spine. Sean never looked at me and made me feel seen, but Deacon? It's like being flayed open. Today, I hate it.

I want to be impenetrable.

"No hugs. I'll break down." I hold my hand up as Deacon steps closer. Instead, he pecks my cheek and presses his forehead against mine. I encircle one hand behind his neck and intentionally slow my breathing, appreciating the calmness his presence brings me.

"You got this. The day will be over before you know it. Take comfort in knowing you're you, and Sean's Sean. You win at the end of the day by that simple fact."

As I giggle slightly, Deacon steps back and shoves his hands in his tuxedo pockets. He's right. At least Sean hadn't changed my character or my heart. I'd emerged from ten years of his haughty heartlessness still equipped with love and compassion, and when the time is right, I'll manage to give my heart again. Healing is inevitable, right?

I won't let Sean wreck me.

"See you in a few," Deacon says, reaching out one last time to stroke my cheek softly with his forefinger. "You'll be alright, Beck."

Beckett is my last name, and only Deacon calls me Beck. I give him a grin that's more enthusiastic than I feel.

"You're right. I will be. Thanks for reminding me of that, and for the vote of confidence. See you soon." We exchange one last smile before I hurry back into the bridal suite and find my friends.

"You may now kiss your bride, Cody," the officiant proclaims. Tara's husband, Cody, takes her into his arms and kisses her deeply. He dips her, nearly knocking her right off her feet, and I hear her sweet giggle as Cody easily tips her back upright. The officiant announces them as a married couple for the first time, and upon hearing her new last name with a "Mrs." in front of it, she shrieks, "Oh my god!" and throws her arms around Cody again.

A chorus of giggles comes from the front row around me, where I'm seated with the rest of the bridesmaids. As Tara passes by, I hand her bouquet back, and the two of them walk back down the aisle as a newly married couple.

Tara pumps her bouquet over her head and sways her hips as they celebrate and dance their way down the red velvet aisle. Despite what's happening in my personal life, my heart swells with joy for Tara and Cody finally saying "I do" to one another. I hope they last forever. They're perfect together. Some couples can go the distance; I still believe that.

My eyes dart around, gazing at my surroundings. We're probably at around 8,000 feet elevation, and the scenery is beautiful, filled with aspen trees, my namesake, just beginning to turn colors as fall approaches.

Behind the venue is a tiny bridge over a creek leading up to narrow trails, and a few people on horseback navigate up the mountain. An abundance of clouds help cover up the unseasonably warm sun, but don't threaten any rain. The sound of fast-moving water mingles with the gentle croaks of distant frogs and the lively birdsong overhead; nature creates a comforting symphony to soothe me. I turn my face to the sky and soak up the peaceful vibes of this gorgeous Saturday.

I'd poured all of myself into Sean for a decade. Even though we'd just ended, there is a promise of something better—something happier—on the horizon, wafting through the clean mountain air. Don't endings usually lead to beginnings? Something tells me I won't be waiting long for mine.

I've got my life together if you don't count my love life— working in my field of bereavement counseling and having great friends, an active social life, and hobbies I enjoy. And with the hope of a new beginning washing over me, I turn to Sean and give him my elbow for the last time, allowing him to escort me down the aisle to a cocktail hour on the lodge's patio. It's scheduled for an hour while Cody and Tara take photos, and then the rest of the bridal party and close family will be beckoned to the clearing by the creek for less intimate photos later.

"Hey, Aspyn!" Deacon's brother, Steele, apprises me warmly from the end of the aisle, and Sean passes me off to him with a look of disgust. He's never approved of my friendship with either of the Ambrose brothers, though he's never outright said it. He just encouraged me to be more of a "girl's girl" and spend time with my girlfriends. Despite coming down on me for having guy friends, Sean had constantly spoken about women at work, and had even been caught texting one inappropriately in the middle of the night. But that's Sean: rules for thee, not for me.

"What a lovely wedding, don't you think?" Steele takes my elbow and leads me toward the bar, which is exactly where I want to go.

"Perfect. Exactly what I want someday, with a man like Cody who values things like warmth, loyalty, and fidelity. Someone who'll cherish me." My smile feels broken. "Maybe fewer guests, just a few of the most beloved. But yes, it was lovely and they make a beautiful couple."

His hand moves to the small of my back as he moves me forward in line to the bar.

He lowers his voice to tell me, "I hear a certain someone hasn't quite lived up to his promises as a partner. Not as into the loyalty bit as you are. I'm sorry to hear about that. And don't worry, I won't tell a soul."

"It's all right. It will come out sooner rather than later." I sigh, then order a Moscow Mule. "How've you been? Haven't heard from you in a while."

"Good. You know, keeping busy. Back at school now, and I miss the summer like hell." Steele cracks a straight smile with his pearly-white teeth and shrugs. "It's what I love doing, though. Oh, don't look, but Sean's glare is burning a hole into your back from behind us. Pretend I said something hilarious."

I lift my face toward Steele and laugh voraciously, tipping my head back and feeling my curls bounce as he joins in. It almost sounds real.

"Shit, he's coming this way," Steele tells me with a grimace only I'm meant to see. Sean comes up behind me and palms my ass, which makes me want to knee him in the balls.

I exhale sharply and whisper, "Get your fucking hand off me or I will bite your fingers off."

"Jesus, woman, have you gone insane?" Sean looks at me like I have three heads.

"Not at all, asshole. I have more clarity than ever. Now, get that scowl off your face. Pretend you're a doting big brother. It's your sister's big day!" I elbow him as Wendy and her boyfriend Jett, who's also Sean's cousin, approach and stand around the tall circular table with us. Steele just sort of sways and looks uncomfortable as he drinks his own Moscow Mule.

Throwing mine back, I'm grateful for the alcohol's burn, and I guzzle it down. Steele grabs my drink and goes off to refill it while we all engage in friendly banter, eventually leading to Jett telling Sean, "Man, you hit the jackpot with Aspyn. She's hilarious, speaks fluent sarcasm, and puts up with your miserable ass. Frankly, she's too good for you. Just like Wendy is way too good for me."

He leans in and kisses Wendy as a dour look crosses Sean's face. He's quiet at least, broody looking, his dark curls carefully coiffed back with gel, dark circles beneath his eyes. He looks like shit, but he deserves to. I hope the pull-out sofa with all its lumps bothered his back all night long. *Asshole.*

Sean could probably sense the daggers shooting out of my eyes as we left the house together and drove up in separate cars. I'd had the urge to crash my Durango into his precious Audi, and I may have, if I hadn't wanted to be on time for hair and makeup. It's not that I'm crazy, emotional, or unhinged—I'm just fucking furious. Furious I wasted ten of my very best years on the biggest dickhead in the whole state of Colorado.

"Well, thanks, Jett. I think he's a fortunate guy too," I utter while a shadow appears on Sean's features. He stays quiet. "No one's luckier than Cody. Did you see his smile when Tara's father walked her down the aisle? I always watch the groom. I've never seen him smile like that before. Talk about knowing how lucky he is. Tara's a catch."

"I saw him, too. Like, he couldn't believe Tara would marry him. That's the look you better have, Jett." Wendy turns her face up and kisses him a few seconds longer than I expect her to.

It's an effort to keep a smile pasted on my face, but in the presence of a couple who truly loves one another, I can't help but let my smile slip for a second. I want what they have, but instead, I have this pissant cheater. Plus, I'm about to start over and build my life from the ground up without the man I'd been with since I was nineteen. It's not that I feel I can't do it, but I'm annoyed that I have to.

Sean had been my first. My only. God only knows how many women Sean has been with during our long relationship. So far, I only know about two, though I'm sure it was more of a pattern than I'd realized.

The first time I caught him texting a gorgeous blonde, he insisted they never met up, and he "just dipped his toes into the water" to see if he was "still desirable." Then, he promptly turned it around on me for making him feel unlovable and undesired. I could never give him enough sex to make him happy. Nurse Q being so ready and hot for his 'giant' dick is much harder for him to talk himself out of. He hadn't tried this morning. I'm sure his affair with her will continue—just a niggling feeling I have. I'd had my suspicions about a coworker of his too, whom I'd caught him texting at 3 a.m., but I'd given him the benefit of the doubt.

"How's the babymaking going?" Wendy asks, sipping her champagne as Steele returns with my refilled drink. My stomach gurgles.

"We've been trying." Sean winks like he wants everyone to know how often we're fucking, which grosses me out so much

I almost throw up into my drink. Gulping hard, the nausea passes.

"You know, sometimes the universe knows what you need and what you don't. We haven't had any success, but I've been checked out, so I think it's probably time to have Sean see his doc, if only to test how strong his swimmers are."

I try to bite back a laugh at my evil admission. There is some truth to it: we didn't try to prevent pregnancy and the doctor had given me an all-clear to start trying last year. It hadn't happened yet, thank gods. Thankfully, Sean would never be between my thighs again, so I figure the gods themselves had spared me from eighteen or more years of attachment to Sean. *Good riddance.*

"That's too bad. Maybe you just need to try harder." Wendy wiggles her eyebrows suggestively while I try not to vomit at the thought.

"I think we're good." I pat her hand on the table and ask if I can refill her champagne. My Mule is gone, so I grab our empties and walk to the bar, where Deacon leans against a nearby tree looking casual and handsome as always.

The sun peeks out from behind the clouds, shining brightly on his tall, muscular figure like a natural spotlight. Squinting into the bright afternoon, I make my way over to him.

"How're you hanging in there?" Deacon asks, raking a hand through his slightly wavy golden hair, before grabbing the empties from me and setting them on the bar.

"Tired of people talking about me and Sean reproducing." I roll my eyes so hard an eyelash dislodges, and I wipe it carefully out of my eye. "Can't believe I ever wanted a baby with a man who doesn't know how to love anyone but his own goddamn self."

"Love blinds." Deacon punctuates his words with a shrug.

"I don't think that's the expression, but it's not far from

the truth." I chuckle, reaching out for Wendy's refill. "Ugh. I should get back over there. You know, to hell. At least your brother is over there making nice. You'd be welcome to join us and talk about anything but fetuses, sperm, or my empty womb."

I point at the table where Sean stands chatting with his cousin. Wendy and Steele appear deep in conversation.

Deacon grabs his whiskey on the rocks and follows me to the table of doom. He stands between me and Sean, with Steele on the other side of me. In this Ambrose sandwich, I finally feel protected from Sean, who's on his phone texting, potentially inquiring about a particular nurse's nether regions.

Deacon suddenly takes a baggie out of his pants pocket. "I forgot to tell you. I was going through my mother's things," his mother had recently passed away from brain cancer, "and I found this funky turquoise ring that screamed your name, Beck. There is a certificate of authenticity stating that it's one of a kind. I think she got it in Sedona. Let me see that finger. Maybe it'll fit."

My head spins when I see the beautiful cushion-shaped turquoise ring, and I reach out my hand, all the while telling him he should keep it to remember her by. Glancing down, he slides it on, a glowing halo of onyx surrounds the center stone, and I'm stunned by its beauty. The ring looks like it was made for me, so I'm not surprised by how well it fits or how perfect it looks on my right hand. Normally, I wouldn't accept such a pricey gift, but it's from Deacon. If he wants me to have his mother's ring, he'll be insulted if I don't accept it.

Plus, oh my god, it's stunning. I spot silver filigree containing tiny diamonds around the entirety of the delicate band and nearly drool.

Opening and closing my mouth like a fish, I shake my head in total awe. Staring down at the ring on my finger, then back up at Deacon, I'm touched by this gift.

"Are you sure? It was your mom's," I whisper. My thumb rubs over the turquoise as I admire it.

"Yes. I don't have sisters. Aunt Louise says she has fat fingers, and I know turquoise is your birthstone and favorite color. It was always meant to be yours. I knew it when I saw it, and Steele has no problem with it either."

Steele stares down at it and nods. "It's nearly as beautiful as you are, my friend." He sets his hand on my shoulder blade and squeezes me gently. My head tilts to his shoulder as my hand hikes into the air, the diamonds glimmering in the sunlight.

Sean opens his mouth like a guppy, but instead of closing it, he just walks away without a word. Good.

Jett calls after him, "Hey, I guess if you don't put a ring on your lady's finger, someone else might!" Jett glances down at the ring and smiles.

"It might be the most thoughtful gift I've ever received," I say, squeezing Deacon's hand tightly at my side.

Wendy and Jett share a private look that seems to exchange words, and I sigh against Steele's shoulder.

"I love it so much, guys. Thank you doesn't express how I feel well enough." I can't stop staring at the ring on my finger, nor remembering Lillian, Steele and Deacon's mother I'd loved so much.

Jett eventually walks away, following Sean, and they seem to be exchanging intense words. I had been hoping Sean wouldn't tell Jett we'd broken up yet, but what else could be happening? Shit. I hadn't wanted to cause a scene on Tara's big day.

"Of course I would give it to you, doll face. You're my best female friend, Beck, and you have the same tiny piano-player fingers Mom had. It was a no-brainer, and there's no need to thank me. It helps to give her favorite things to people she loved, and she loved you. I have so much more I'd like you to go through. You were also about the same size, and she was a fashionista right until the end."

Wendy frowns. "Steele, Deac, I'm so sorry, again. Your mom was my favorite of Jett's aunts. She always made me feel welcome on the holidays and at all the family gatherings." Wendy and Jett had been dating for years, and we all became fast friends after the first couple of months.

"Maybe I can help determine what you should sell and what to give away," I tell the guys, formulating a plan to help them go through Lillian's closet. Deacon squeezes my hand and agrees, but Steele insists that I go through it first, call all my dibs, and then get the rest of the girls over to have them dive into the closet too. It's a good plan, and they shouldn't have to go through her things alone.

Someone whistles off in the distance, which I suppose means we're off to take photos. Reluctantly, I walk toward the clearing where Tara and Cody stand surrounded by family and wonder how I'm going to play this one.

When it finally comes time to take photos, the day gets uncomfortable. The family insists I pose for photos with them, even though I'm already in all the bridesmaid photos, and I politely insist they take at least a few without me. I end up allowing myself to be in just a couple of them.

Tara and Sean's mother, Cecile, looks right through me and gives me a frown. Beside me, she whispers, "I'm sorry. You'll always be family to me." She knows, though no one else seems to notice.

Deacon and Steele are also featured in the family photos, as they'd been honorary Wright family members since high school, when they first met Sean. Deacon's mother had asked the boys to make themselves scarce after school while she taught piano lessons, so they'd ended up with the Wrights most days, and they'd practically adopted the brothers.

How could I think I'd get Deacon and Steele in the breakup? They had more history with the Wrights than I did. I didn't meet them in college until after I'd met Sean, and they'd pledged the same fraternity. That's how I met them, one night at a frat party. Sean had introduced himself to me first, back in my pink hair days.

I look down at the ring on my right index finger and breathe deeply. Would Deacon have given me this ring if he intended to side with Sean and dip out of my life without a backward glance?

Would he want me to have his mother's things? Probably not.

Deacon stands by Sean, who's still being his shitty self, and he rests his hand on Sean's shoulder for the photo, providing a convincing enough smile. Still, I see the shadow on Deac's face. He's not happy to be in this photo either.

Finally, Deacon beckons to me for the last group photo, and he puts his arm around me as I stand between him and Steele, with Sean behind me, not daring to touch me. After a few blinding flashes, the group breaks up, but not before Cecile wraps me in her arms, whispering to me to call her in a few days.

"Let's blow this joint," Deacon tells me, wrapping an arm around my waist and leading me toward the little bridge over the creek behind us. Thankfully, Tara had insisted we all wear Converse to her wedding, so I'm in comfortable shoes while we carefully traverse to the center of the bridge.

Leaning over the creek, I peer into the clear water to count the fish near the surface. Some of them jump up and out of the water.

"I wish I had my fishing pole." I reach into the pocket of my dress—*yes, it has pockets*—and grab a hair tie. My perfectly curled light-brown golden hair is beginning to fall flat anyway, so I quickly make a fishtail braid over my shoulder and tie it off.

"It's astonishing how quickly you make such an intricate braid." Deacon has his phone out, and I get the weird sense he may have just taken a photo of me. When he leans forward to show it to me, he smiles and says, "See how gorgeous you look today?"

I laugh it off and tell him, "I've always been good with knots. Dad taught me young. Gosh, I miss him." Their house in the mountains sits empty without them. Eventually, I had hoped Sean and I would move into it along with the family we created, but in the meantime, I use it as an Airbnb.

The money I pocket from it has helped me repay my student loans, pay off my Durango, and still have some fun money left over. I use some of it to pay for a housekeeper to take care of the sprawling house before and after visitors come. Now, I have no choice but to move back and live in the monstrous house alone until I decide what to do next. My parents always intended for me to have their house, but it's too big for just me.

"How are your parents doing? Have you told them about the breakup?"

I groan. "They rarely call. I'm the one who reaches out to them, and you know the time difference with Japan is ridiculous. I can't believe Dad is refusing to retire from his cushy Marine's job. He should leave it up to the younger guys, you know? Mom only moved a few years ago when she was certain I was stable with Sean, and I'm afraid to tell them how Sean has let them down. Mom trusted him to take care of me, and look how well that turned out, huh?"

"I'm sorry. What's next, Beck?"

"Well, I guess I'll escape to Mom and Dad's mountain home, but I have it booked with Airbnb guests for the next few weeks. I'll wait things out at Sean's until then. I'm in no hurry to relinquish the property to him, anyway."

I tip my face up to the sky to look at the puffy, picture-like clouds. One looks like a turtle overhead, while another reminds me of a bear. It feels so good to be away from Sean, but I'm morose about losing the family I'd come to view as my own. Knowing they won't be my family for long makes my heart feel torn and empty.

Who would I have now? What would I do on holidays?

"With your parents in Japan, I know Sean's family kind of became yours," Deacon says as if he's reading my mind. "Must be difficult to know that it may not last, with blood being thickest and all."

I frown, my throat tightening with the sobs I'm trying to hold back, so I clear it a few times. Two hot tears fall from just one eye, and I blink back the rest.

"Yeah. I think that might be the hardest part. I'm an only child, and I've enjoyed being part of such a big clan. They're all lovely and welcoming. Cecile is like a second mother to me, as was your mom."

"Hey, you'll still have my dad and my big, crazy family. With five male siblings, I've got enough family to go around. Of course, they're older and have families now, and our gatherings surely include a lot of diaper changes, toddlers fighting, and heating of bottles."

I smile. "I love that, Deac. Your family is fantastic. I especially adore Steele, you know that." I glance back down at the reception, and I spot Steele, since he stands a solid three inches taller than everyone else there. He's a great guy, one year older than Deacon, and he teaches fifth-grade science to a bunch of kids he views as his own. He's not much for relationships and hasn't brought a girl around in the longest time.

"Steele loves you, too. They all do." Deacon pushes a stray strand of hair behind my ear.

"So why aren't your sisters-in-law desperate to get hold of Lillian's jewelry and accessories?"

"They were all willed to me and Steele. Aunt Louise got a lot of her clothes, but she asked me to take care of them since the grief was too fresh for her, so I agreed. It's a daunting task for two bachelors." Deacon shrugs, but I know the topic is painful.

Reaching out and throwing my arm around Deacon's waist, I lean against him. "I get that and will help if I can. Deac? This ring..." It stares up at me, twinkling. "It's astounding. Are you really going to turn against Sean after being friends for so long? Just because of what he did to me?"

"Beck, it's not just what he did to you. He's slime in a way he didn't used to be. It's simple, choosing you. Sean hasn't been the greatest friend lately anyway, not like he was in high school and college, and I've been closer to you than him for years. Hell, half the time I call, you end up picking up his phone anyway, and you're the one I come to with my problems. Of course, it's going to be you, Beck, and Sean is no big loss. Not for me, and certainly not for you."

"I'll take one of those bear hugs now," I whisper. When Deacon surrounds me in his arms, I finally let myself cry.

"I can't believe he did this," I sniffle, hating that the tears are over a tool like Sean. "I think he may have been cheating for most of our relationship."

As a bereavement counselor and friend, I should try to get Deacon to open up about his mom's passing, not make him comfort me over my idiot ex. I let Deacon hold me for a few minutes before I dry my tears and refuse to feel sorry for myself any longer.

"Let's hike. Nothing too strenuous, but it'll help us, being out in nature. I doubt we'll be missed." Deacon grabs my elbow and points me toward the peaks behind us. He knows just what I need.

Thankfully, my dress is party length rather than an evening gown, and it's not too tight to move in. Though, it'll be the first dress I've ever hiked in, but there's a first time for everything.

5

ASPYN

I take off following Deacon as he ascends the steep trail above us, and we hike in companionable silence until dusk smears orange and pink streaks across the sky like finger paints. Peace creeps in, the sorer my calves get.

Losing daylight, we return to the creek, but not before we sit down and see a million stars twinkle in the clear sky overhead. The outdoor dance floor in the distance is lit with white party lights, and reluctantly, we make our way over.

It seems like everyone is dancing or swaying, except Sean, who sits pouting at an empty table not far away. I hate his self-pity more than anything else, and the thought of facing him right now makes my stomach clench and roll.

Turning away, I glance up at Deacon, and his baby blues shine back at me. I can't help but lose myself in them for a few brief moments.

"C'mon," he says, leading me to the dance floor.

We both kick off our shoes and join our dirty hands in mid-slow dance as Deanna Carter sings about young love and innocence. Ignoring everyone's stares as we sway in each other's arms, I feel safe and content against Deacon's chest. We are sweatier than everyone else and a lot more sober, but after the dance, we catch up by doing a few tequila shots together at the bar and then head back out to the dance floor. When Deacon puts his hands on my hips and uses them to move me around the dance floor, the butterflies intensify until I'm breathless. His hands on my body feel good, and when he pushes a stray strand of curled hair behind my ear, my heart speeds up.

What on earth is happening tonight?

I glance up at the full moon and blame it on her silvery-blue beauty and the chaos she brings with her.

Around eleven-thirty, Tara finds me at the bar, and she asks me with wide eyes, "Is it over with you two, then? You haven't danced together once."

The alarm on her face breaks my heart, and I try to calm my trembling upper lip. I want to burst into tears and tell her I hadn't been able to make Sean loyal to me, and apologize that we'll never be sisters-in-law, as we both have always wanted.

"Tara, honey, I didn't want to ruin your night. This is a day you'll never have again. Why don't we talk more when you get back from Jamaica?" I rest my hand on her shoulder and give her a small, comforting smile.

"But you're the sister I always wanted!" Tara's eyes fill with tears, and she leans forward to hug me tightly. "What did my brother do?"

With a sigh— "He cheated."

"That fuck!" Tara practically shouts.

I shush her as she curses her brother the same way I want to.

"I just don't understand. When someone finds a woman like you, they're supposed to hold on to her. Not fuck around with other people. You're the best he could ever do!"

Her words heat me and comfort me. "Thanks for that, honey. Please don't let this bring you down tonight. You have one handsome husband to go dance with. And things will change, Tara, but don't let him force you to cut me out. When you get home, I want to see all your photos and videos and hear about the honeymoon, okay? I hope it's the best time of your life. You're a perfect bride, girl."

I smooth away a few stray strands of hair and wipe a black mascara tear from her face. "Go back to your hubby and dance!" I command her. "Don't worry even a little bit about me."

Finally, Tara obeys, and I lean against the bar with a heavy sigh.

"Well, that sucked," the bartender sighs from behind me, startling me. His name tag says, "Anders."

"It was hard to pretend I was still with her brother when I couldn't even look him in the eye all day." I roll my eyes.

"So, you're not dating the tall blond dude with the musculature of Thor?" Anders asks, pouring me another tequila while I laugh and explain that Deacon is just a friend.

As I talk with Anders, he flirts, and I throw back a few more shots, which is probably what leads to my final act of the evening—stumbling upstairs to the rooms and putting my key card in front of every door that starts with a "22," hoping to find my room through blurry vision.

"What are you doing here?" I ask as the door lock lights up green and lets me in. I'd temporarily forgotten that Anders was following me up here, and I'm confused when he follows me into the room.

"You asked me if I wanted to fuck. I said hell yeah. I thought that was pretty clear," Anders chuckles. He grabs my braid and tugs me closer with it. Anders kisses me deeply, all tongue, as a fog descends over me, my ability to say no depleted.

"Let me help you with this dress," Anders says, reaching around my body and tugging it down.

"Out!" A stern voice shouts.

I open my eyes, my body swaying as my gaze finally focuses on Deacon, who reiterates, "I said out!"

Anders holds up his hands. "She asked me, man!"

"Consider yourself unasked!"

"Goodnight," Anders calls as he turns and walks away.

Deacon shuts the door. "You'll just feel worse about yourself if you sleep with him tonight," Deacon stands in front of me with his tie unknotted most of the way, looking disheveled but beautiful. "And you're so drunk, you can't consent, anyway."

"I can't get my dress off," I whine, reaching back for the zipper that Anders must have re-zipped. "I'm sweaty and so uncomfortable! And-and you...you ruined my fun!" I don't mention, mere seconds ago, I had forgotten about the "fun" I wanted to have, overlooking the fact that I had a plus one chasing after me up to the room.

Deacon unzips my dress, letting it plunge to the floor, and then he helps me step out of it without tripping. I feel vulnerable in front of him in nothing but a strapless nude bra and matching underwear. Not that he'd never seen me in a skimpier bikini—I had people over to my parents' place all the time for swimming parties, but this feels different somehow. More intimate. Dangerous, even.

"You get cozy. I'll grab your suitcase. I'm taking your extra room key, and I'll be right back." Deacon hands me cold water, commands me to drink it, and then he disappears. Shrugging off my bra, I climb into bed, tugging the sheet up slightly. My head spins as I finally close my eyes and drift off.

A few minutes later, I feel a presence and open my eyes. They take a while to focus, but I sit up after realizing Deacon's at my bedside.

"Hi."

"Take these," Deacon orders, handing me three pills.

Obeying without a second thought, I swallow the pain reliever with the rest of my water, realizing suddenly I am topless, sitting up against the headboard on full display for Deacon.

"Shit," I groan, pulling the sheet up and giving Deacon an apologetic look. "Oh, thanks for not letting me fuck Anders."

"You're welcome. Do you want me to grab your pajamas?" Deacon asks, but I'm too tired, so I just collapse on the bed.

"I'm nearby. See you in the morning. I have your spare room key, so I'll get you up."

"Stay," I whisper, not wanting to be alone tonight.

"No. Not with you half-naked." Deacon laughs. "I don't want anyone to think I took advantage of your drunkenness. That's not the kind of man I am."

"I *know* what kind of man you are." It's nearly a whisper.

Deacon is the perfect man. All-American, tall, athletic, intelligent, and charismatic, with a great sense of humor. His body looks like he's spent his life in the gym, but nothing could be further from the truth.

Deac is all about the outdoors. He loves rock climbing, flag football, and pickup hockey games in the winter. Naturally athletic, always on the move, down for whatever, whenever, when it comes to sports and outdoor activities. And I could be counted on to make lots of hot cocoa for those hockey games, or lemonade in the summer. Rock-climbing, well, no thanks. I'm not up for scaling mountains—I'm not nearly that kind of adrenaline junkie, though I will happily hike up one.

"Then you already know I'm going to park it here in this chair, wait twenty seconds for you to fall asleep, and come back with more aspirin for you in the morning."

I smile, already knowing that's the case, and then turn to

my side, facing away from him. Feeling secure and warm, a dreamless sleep captures me.

6
DEACON

It's 3 a.m., and I can't sleep. I'm too busy having all these feelings that I should not feel for a woman who belonged to my best friend until yesterday. She hadn't helped matters by sitting half-nude in my presence, making me confront those pesky feelings. Maybe I can blame it on hormones, but I'm not a pubescent boy. Blame it on the magical wedding making me feel all romantic and shit.

What I feel is wrong on so many levels.

My dick is hard, either again or still, I'm not sure, but when I close my eyes, it's Beck's dusky-pink nipples and round, perky breasts I see in my mind, and my stomach swirls with disgust at myself.

It had taken everything in me to exit her room after she fell headlong into a deep sleep, snores and all. And yeah, I'm a good guy, but the temptation had been great. My ass remained in that chair, staring at her slim, muscular back for nearly an hour, guarding her and pondering my feelings for her. Now sleep won't come.

I feel restless and confused. To some extent, I must admit to myself that these feelings have always been inside me; I'd just buried them deep enough, I thought they would never surface. But now that Beck is a free woman, the adoration I feel for her clobbers me over the head. Though, I know I can't let on what I feel, especially during this vulnerable time in her life, when she's heartbroken over Sean's infidelity and overall douchebaggery.

The truth is, I want to break his neck for what he's done to her in their entire relationship. I'd never seen a woman so faithful, so loving, as Beck had always been to Sean, and that fucker hadn't deserved it from the first second they met. He'd done nothing but fall short of deserving her every moment of their relationship. Between his hectic on-call schedule he couldn't help and total lack of giving a shit about her being at home waiting on him, Sean was unavailable and unreliable at best.

I can't count the number of times Sean went out with the guys to hit the bars or clubs and flirted excessively with other women. Danced with them, far too close, touched them intimately, all while ignoring Beck's texts. I made a habit of letting Beck know when we were leaving at night, which annoyed Sean in case he wanted to keep the party going somewhere else. Or with someone else. At her place, of course, never his.

I'd suspected he cheated—not once or twice, as Beck seems to think, but frequently. It's a struggle not to blame myself. I should have told Beck to stop wasting her twenties on Sean, should have told Sean more often to be better, but I just hung back and let it play out. Now I feel like a piece of shit about it.

Someone should have been looking out for Beck. Putting her first.

So, I will, from now on.

Finally, merciful sleep gives me a reprieve from my self-flagellation.

When my alarm goes off a few hours later, I brush my teeth, comb my hair, and throw on slacks and a light blue button-down. I grab the aspirin and another water out of the minibar, and I let myself into her room right across the hallway.

Beck's on top of the sheet, mostly naked except for a pair of skimpy panties, and I don't know how to look away. Still, I try to be noble. Reaching for the blanket rolled up at the bottom of the bed, I pull it up over her and set the water and three more pills on the bedside table. Next, I grab her phone and set an alarm to make sure she doesn't miss the going-away brunch.

I perch with my shoulder on the doorframe, just watching Beck for a minute. Her light-brown hair is kissed by the sun, causing blonde streaks to dance through it. It's messy and covers much of her face, and I long to reach out and tame the silky locks for her.

Beck sleeps with her mouth closed, and she breathes heavily in and out through her nose, which is dotted with the perfect number of freckles that also stretch across her cheekbones from all her time in the sun. She's beautiful—stunning, even in sleep. Maybe even more so when she sleeps, so peacefully. With all the gentleness I can muster, I glide my fingertips beneath the hair in her eyes and smooth it back so I can see the entirety of her face.

I reach down and smooth my thumb over the front of her hand, catching a glance at the cushion-shaped turquoise ring that had once sparkled on my mother's hand. It's right that it's here with Beck. It suits her spunky, Bohemian personality, and Mom would be thrilled to know it ended up Beck's.

When she groans and pulls a pillow over her head, I roll my eyes at myself for admiring Beck for so long.

Finally, I stand, take a backward glance at the beauty

sleeping in the lodge bed, and let myself out of her room and back into my own.

Why is my heart thumping wildly in my chest? It's just Beck. The woman I'd been friends with for a decade.

The one I'd laid eyes on first. My foot wants to kick something, but this room is too well-appointed to take my frustration out on it, so I just breathe through the recollection of the first time I laid eyes on Aspyn Beckett and tell myself that things always happen the way they're meant to.

Back when we'd met, I was still a kid. Now, I'm a man with strong shoulders for her to cry on, and a deep longing to take care of her in a way only a man can.

With a start, I realize Beck is everything to me. Maybe she always has been.

And this is what they call being up shit's creek.

❧ 7 ❧

ASPYN

"You want to tell me exactly what's going on between you and my best friend Deacon?"

Sean's voice is loud. And close. Way too close. How did he even get in here? *Jesus Christ.*

My head twinges with pain as I sit up and look around, bleary-eyed. He's shoved open the curtains, blinding me, so I press my fists against my eyes and shudder at his presence.

"When you weren't paying attention, he became my best friend, not yours." I pull the sheet up over my breasts and lean against the headboard, as dismissive as possible.

"Oh, we'll see about that." He waves his hand like he's got it handled.

"Shut the fucking curtains, Sean."

After waiting a few seconds, he finally yanks them closed and sits down beside the bed with a grunt-like noise that betrays no emotion.

"You can't really tell me you're leaving me. We've been together for a decade. You don't want this. Just last week, you wanted my baby, didn't you? 'Put a baby in me, Sean,' you said." Sean snorts, his tone haughty and sarcastic.

"Well, a lot can change in a week, and now I don't want to even look at you, much less make you a father." I shrug, grabbing another bottle of water that had appeared beside the bed, probably from Deacon last night. I spot more round pills and pop the aspirin on an empty stomach.

"It seems you have no shortage of wet pussies to fit your *giant* cock into, so it feels like the right time for me to tell you to go do that instead of bothering me." I send him daggers with my eyes.

"What's a little sexting? Come on. You're being unreasonable. I didn't cheat on you with that nurse. She's nothing to me. A conquest at best." His casual eye roll makes me want to throat-punch him.

"This is about your pattern of disrespect for me. People in relationships don't look up cam girls on the internet to get off. They don't sext women they work with. They don't engage in long-term texting and meet-ups behind their lover's back. I let the first one slide because I didn't have proof, but now I see the pattern, Sean, and I won't let you do it to me again. You may think you can walk all over me forever, but that ends now." Proud of my firm voice, I give him a little close-lipped smile.

"I knew you were holding on to that Jocelyn situation! You let that make you so crazy. We were just co-workers. She was going through a hard time and needed someone to talk to." The worst part is how sincere Sean sounds, even though he is undoubtedly lying.

"Oh, and you're the right person for that? You're no knight in shining armor, Sean. And I'm not crazy. She was messaging you in the middle of the night. Innocent people don't text at three in the morning! Get out of my room." My anger ratchets until I'm not sure I can avoid throwing the throat-punch he so deeply deserves. My hands shake from holding back.

"You think I'm going to let you take my best friend from me?" Sean speaks so levelly, I almost don't catch how angry he is. The dude is ice cold; how had I stayed with him for so long? Much less have wanted him to be a father to my child?

"I don't think you have any say in the matter. You've been a shitty friend and a shittier partner, so you'll lose who you need to lose until you learn your lessons. Or until you don't. Either way, I won't be here for it. Now get the fuck out of here, Sean, and if I see you at the house today for any reason but to pack your bags, I'm going to make your life a living hell, like you've made mine for a decade." I clench and wring my hands, mainly to keep them from turning into fists.

"If you're going to be a crazy bitch, I don't want to be there, anyway. You have exactly thirty days. I'm changing the locks on day thirty-one."

"Oh, right, I forgot that I'm always the crazy bitch. Well, you're the *cheating* bitch, Sean, and I have abundant proof. If you think you are going to take the moral high ground here and blame it on me, I'll send everyone screenshots, and people at the hospital might respect you a bit less. So, I can make this easy on you or hard for you, only you get to choose. If you don't get out of this room right now, I will absolutely choose the hard way. That's a fucking promise." I force myself to stare into his eyes with just the right amount of 'crazy bitch' in my glare.

Sean slams the door on his way out without another word, and I finally exhale. We were no strangers to fighting and *crazy bitch* isn't exactly a new phrase for him to throw around, so I let it roll off my back.

I need to make an appearance at breakfast in—I glance at the clock—an hour and then tiptoe out of there without making a scene. That's the goal. Fly under the radar as best I can, keep the bride and groom in the limelight, and definitely no throat-punching Sean.

My hands again curl into fists that want so badly to be used. I tell them, "I know, but it's Tara's day to shine, not ours." I force myself to stretch my hands out in front of me, letting out a sigh. I've got one hell of a right cross, a target acquired, but the wrong damn timing.

A knock comes at the door, and I hear a little beep. It opens to Deacon standing there, leaning against the doorway with an unreadable expression on his face.

Finally, he sighs. "Your tits are out, doll face." He turns the other direction and puts his hand over his eyes.

"Oops. Sorry." I walk from the bed to the table where my suitcase is spread out, and rummage in it until I find a ruffle-sleeved teal dress that works perfectly for the early-fall occasion. Deacon averts his eyes while I dress.

"Alright, all good. I've officially broken up with Sean, by the way. The bastard was just in here calling me a crazy bitch and telling me if I think I get you in our breakup, I'm even crazier." My eye twitches with remembrance. "I still don't know how he got in here."

"I'm in the room across the hall, so I heard a little bit of that. I didn't like his tone. Frankly, I never have. Not before it ended or after."

I run a brush through my messy hair, the remaining light brown curls loosening into barely there waves, and I secure it into a braid while Deacon sits at the desk chair, looking at me in awe. "I still don't get how you women do things like braiding. I tried it on my niece's My Little Pony, and it was pathetic. Paisley laughed at me. Laughed like a hyena, and so did my sister-in-law."

I giggle, grabbing my makeup bag and heading to the bathroom.

"I like that, Beck."

Puzzled, I ask, "What do you like?"

"You laughing. I want to hear you do more of that."

Deacon appears in the doorway, watching me line my hazel eyes with brown liquid. I add a rosy pop of color to my eyelids and use the same color on my cheeks.

"So, how bad is the hangover?" Deacon asks.

"Oh, ha. It's there. Though the aspirin has kicked in, so thanks for that. Just need to get some food into my stomach to cushion those meds without making a scene down there." I frown, thinking that this may be the last time I'm in the same room with all these people at once—people I'd once called my family.

"Hey, it'll be fine, okay? We'll sit with friends, not with the family." Deacon continues staring at me in the mirror as I fuss over myself.

"I already told Tara. She guessed it, so I just confirmed she was on the right track. Wonder if she spread it around to everyone." I shrug one shoulder like I don't care, my lips pulling into a line as I sigh noisily because I do care, and I hate that I care.

"Sean acting like a pissed-off teenager is probably a clue-in as well. That little bitch." Deacon leans in and wipes a little smudge of eyeliner below my bottom lash line, and we look into each other's eyes a bit too deeply as he wipes it away. The touch does something to my body that it shouldn't, though I refuse to dwell on it.

"He insists he didn't cheat. He still won't cop to it, even though I have irrefutable proof." Chuckling, I shake my head, digging in my bag for the right lipstick. "But of course, he's lying. He has a tell. He rubs his temple like I'm giving him a headache. I can't believe I just figured this out recently. He does it to make me think I'm crazy and annoying. Hell, maybe the last ten years, I've been every bit as crazy as he thinks I am for having stayed with him. Sean never respected me. Not like I deserved."

I'm angry and sad at the same time. Sorry for wasting all

that time, all that youth I'll never get back. Youth is short and fickle, and already, thirty is approaching, which makes me feel like a feather drifting along the wind who should be grounded somewhere instead. All the expectations I'd had of thirty—marriage, babies—have melted away. The future is nothing but a question mark.

"My mother would be so glad to hear you two broke up," Deacon tells me, running his fingers gently over my braid and tugging on it.

"Really?" I'm aghast. Everyone had seemed to like Sean, including Lillian. That was part of why I liked him so much when we met. He was Mr. Popularity at his fraternity, and he'd overlooked much hotter, sluttier girls and zeroed in on me that night at the party. Or at least, that's what I had thought.

"She always told me you were settling for Sean. You know, she never much liked him. Mom was an excellent judge of character, and she had a very high opinion of you. She wanted you to be with the best man for you—a truly good man—and she knew that wasn't Sean."

I groan, exasperated. "Damn, I wish Lillian had told me that when she was alive." I swallow a lump in my throat and sip my water to clear it. "We did have a kind of weird conversation toward the end, where she talked to me about spreading my wings and finding my greatest life. It was all very confusing, and I wasn't sure what she meant."

"She wasn't one for drama or speaking out of turn." Deacon shrugs.

"Neither are you. I think she'd be so proud of the man you turned out to be. I hope she told you that regularly." I place my hands on Deacon's shoulders and rub them through his linen-blend, light-blue button-down. As a real estate attorney, Deacon has all the most handsome suits, and he looks incredible in them.

"She wanted me to make time for love, not work so much. That much she told me at the end."

"That sounds like her." I smile in remembrance, thinking of how Lillian appeared before she lost her hair and became so sick from radiation and chemo. I can recall her easy, bright smile and her sea-blue eyes, the same color she'd passed to Deacon. Whenever Lillian was around, you just knew everything would be okay. She had this level-headed calmness about her, and she gave excellent advice. Much better than my own mother did.

I think of the Christmas gifts she so carefully wrapped and decorated with perfect bows and the little handmade cards she'd purchased from a tiny shop in Vail. She had always been so thoughtful in her gift-giving, insisting on shopping for every female at the Wrights' famous holiday party on Christmas Eve.

Thankfully, it's only September. I have some time before I spend the holidays alone or overseas in Japan.

I press my hand into Deacon's shoulder and whisper, "I miss her too."

Deacon leans his forehead to mine. We both close our eyes, together remembering Lillian, who, if life were fair at all, would be here today to celebrate with Tara and Cody. She'd have cheered the loudest as they danced back down the aisle into the rest of their lives.

I startle awake, having fallen back to sleep after spending some of the early morning with Beck. My suit is rumpled, and the sun is streaming in through the curtains at the fancy ski lodge Tara and Cody just got married in.

With a groan, I get up and search the room. For some unfair reason, there's not a coffee pot anywhere, so, half-asleep, I change into silver basketball shorts and a black T-shirt before I amble down the stairs to the lobby, letting the smell of coffee lead me in the right direction.

On the way, I run into Sean talking to Cody. They're practically in front of the Keurig machine, so I mutter something about them being in the way, and they move a couple of feet. Still, I hear everything they discuss in hushed tones.

"It's not me, man," Sean tells Cody. "She just says that to deflect from the fact that she can't seem to get pregnant. I've been tracking her cycles and everything, but it never amounts to anything. I think she might have PCOS, or maybe she's just infertile. How can I be expected to stay with someone who can't bear children? You want to be a father as much as I do, so you know how much it means."

I see red as my skin crawls, and I fiddle longer than I need to with sugar and creamers while continuing to overhear the fucked-up conversation.

"You haven't even tried IVF. You shouldn't give up on her for this reason alone," Cody urges Sean like the good guy he is. "I mean, that's a ten-year relationship, buddy—an entire decade. You should fight for her. Aspyn's a good egg who deserves for you to hang in there."

I can't hold back any longer, since I know the truth. And I hate the lies Sean's telling about Beck almost as much as I hate him right now.

"You're such a lying little fuck," I seethe at Sean. "She's got the all-clear from her doctor. You're the problem, man. And if your swimmers could swim, it still wouldn't matter, because Aspyn won't put up with a cheater. She's too good of a woman to sit at home while you stick your dick in anyone you can reach."

I want to spit at him, but this lodge is far too nice for my behavior to devolve that way.

"Oh, you got a problem with me, huh? I thought you might." Sean's voice is full of venom as he lifts all five feet ten inches of himself onto tiptoes to make himself look bigger. He's still five inches shorter than me even with his chest puffed out.

"Oh yes, I have a problem with pathetic, pipsqueak cheaters who lie about their ex's fertility and make drama the morning after a beautiful wedding. Cody, this has nothing to do with you, man, so step back."

He obeys just as I wind back my arm and send a right cross straight to his left eye. I don't hit him hard enough to break bones, but I'm sure he'll have a black eye, and that's what I want—for him to remember this moment every day for the next two weeks.

"Ouch! What the fuck, Deacon?" Sean steps back and grasps his eye with a howl.

"Your ex?" Cody's slow on the uptake.

"She broke up with him the night before your wedding after she found him chatting with a Nurse Q. Did she tell you how wet she was for you, Sean? Is that all it took? A willing, wet pussy to cheat on the best woman you'll ever have? The greatest woman you ever let get away?" I chuckle. "Do us all a favor and get the fuck out of here. We don't want to upset Tara with your black eye."

"Who's Nurse Q?" Cody demands to know as he gets in Sean's face. "How could you cheat on Aspyn, Sean? She's put up with all of your bullshit for ten years!"

Sean shoves Cody out of his way and storms off, still clutching his eye. I wince as I rub my right knuckles with my left hand and wonder if I should have kneed him in the balls instead. It would have hurt him more and hurt me less.

Whatever. It was worth it.

"You really stood up for Aspyn's honor," Cody tells me, proudly. "I mean, look. Sean's my brother-in-law, so he'll be in my life a long time, but if what you're saying is true, he deserved the hell out of that punch and he knows it. We're all good, brother. Let me find you some ice."

I sit down in the lobby, glad no one on staff saw the sucker punch I gave Sean, and my heart races. It strikes me as odd how easy it had been to throw that punch at my former best friend.

Cody materializes with a zipper bag full of ice, and I take it gratefully. It's not that I hate Sean, I just know exactly what he is. He's not good, and he's not worthy of Beck, the dream girl. Anyone's dream girl, really. She fishes, hikes, plays ball, hangs out with the boys, and then gets glammed up to go out with the girls. She has social graces, makes everyone feel comfortable, and then she can out-burp the guys at a barbecue. Beck's the whole package.

After I ice my hand and chat with Cody for a minute, I head up to her room and knock.

She throws the door open and then looks me up and down. "Deacon, where's your suit? And why is your hand bleeding?"

"Oh, it's bleeding? No big deal." I shrug as she opens the door and steps aside to let me in. "Just wanted to update you. Shitface was downstairs in the lobby when I went down for coffee, and he was telling Cody how you're unable to get pregnant. You're the problem; you might have PCOS, or maybe you're just infertile, but he doesn't think he can stay with you if you can't get pregnant. I saw fit to step in, set the record straight, and uh, well, he got the punch that's been coming to him for a while now."

Beck's eyes widen, and her mouth drops open. "You didn't! You did? You really hit him?"

"Punched the motherfucker." I shrug like it's no big deal, and I'm taken aback when Beck grabs me behind my head and kisses me hard on the cheek. When she releases me, she grabs my hand and peers down at it. She shows the right amount of sympathy, but then asks, "How does Sean's face look?"

"Different," I offer. Beck laughs uproariously, bending down, her hands on her waist as she tries to catch her breath.

I touch her back. "I don't think you'll have to see that twit at brunch. I'm sure he's taken his damaged pride and bruised eye home by now. Now, you can go and just relax. Cody's on your side, by the way. He witnessed everything."

Beck blows out a breath. "So, everyone knows we broke up."

"Everyone knows you ended it with him because he's

slime," I correct her. "I still can't believe he told Cody you're infertile. How low can you go?" I snarl as I shake my head angrily.

Beck says something I can't distinguish because I am too busy staring at her beautiful face.

"Sorry, what?" I ask.

"Would you like some Neosporin and bandages? That's the fourth time I've asked, you space cadet."

Beck gets on her knees in front of me as I sit on the edge of the tub and she holds my hand in her warm one. She applies some ointment on the cut on my hand, blows on it to help it dry, and then puts on a bandage that probably won't stay on my knuckle. I try not to let my breath hitch when she leans in and kisses my cheek, this time slowly enough that if I turned my head even slightly, our mouths would meet.

"Thank you," she whispers. "I wanted to punch him myself, but I just got my nails done."

I chuckle and take a chance, pulling her into my arms as I stand up, giving her a long hug. She smells like strawberries and every other delicious thing. "You're welcome. He practically punched himself."

Beck walks me out, and I slip into my room and throw on a gray suit with blue pinstripes on our way downstairs. Beck claims to have forgotten something, and she tells me she'll meet me down there.

When I get downstairs, I glance at the trash can beside the door to the brunch and spot the seating assignment placards in it, then wonder what the hell that's about, especially as I see we're free to sit anywhere. Barry, who goes by Bear and is one of my closest friends, is seated at a table with his girlfriend Marissa, so I head over and take a seat with a muttered "Good morning."

"Hear you fucked Sean up," Marissa tells me. "The rumor

is he was telling people that Aspyn is infertile? What the heck is going on with those two?"

"There's no more 'those two,' because they broke up. And yeah, I punched him because he had it coming. You don't spread lies like that about someone who's been nothing but the best partner to your lousy ass for the last decade."

"Respect." Bear fist bumps my good hand.

I shrug. I'm no hero. A hero wouldn't have enjoyed it as much as I did.

Marissa's face lights up. "Oh, I also heard you jumped in last night when your *friend* Aspyn was about to hook up with the hot bartender."

"He's not hot." I roll my eyes.

"You've always had a hero complex," Marissa tells me.

"Yeah, true," Emmett says as he sits down across from Bear, before silence descends across the table.

"What's going on?" I hear the unmistakable sound of Beck's sweet, clear voice as she floats over to the table in her pretty teal dress, with my mother's turquoise ring blinging out her finger.

"Is everyone talking about me?" Beck asks with a groan, burying her face in her hands. "What? You guys think I'm a slut or something? Yes, I almost hooked up with the bartender, but who wouldn't? He looks like a young Milo Ventimiglia."

"Exactly!" Marissa announces triumphantly. "They don't think he's hot, but I'm with you, girl. I think you would have had fun hooking up with him, and it seems like Deacon crashed your party. That's all I'm trying to say. You're an adult."

"I didn't—" I say at the same time Beck says, "He didn't crash my party. Getting intoxicated and fucking a stranger wouldn't have helped me feel better about the end of my relationship with Sean. Hell, I probably would've blacked out in the middle, anyway."

"You had a lot of tequila, from what I saw," Bear says. "Hell, fine. I admit, I'm the one who saw you throwing back shots with the bartender and then leaving with him and mentioned it to Deacon. I'm sorry about that."

"You did? Why?" Marissa demands to know, glaring at Bear.

"Someone had to look out for her—" Bear starts.

"It's fine, thanks. He stopped me from making a mistake, which I appreciate. How about we move the hell on?" Beck suggests with a dolphin smile and raises her eyebrows high as if she's defying anyone to disagree with her.

"Listen," Marissa says. "It's all about what you want to do, my friend. And if you want to do the bartender, nobody should stop you. Oh, he's filling up mimosa pitchers and topping off Bloody Mary's in the back if you want to say hi. It's not too late for a hookup. You deserve it after everything Sean put you through."

"Or I can go get her a pitcher of mimosas and she won't even have to see him."

"Thanks. Would love some. You don't think anyone will approach me about Sean, do you?" She seems to address all of us.

"Probably not." I move to stand and walk to the table where Anders is filling drinks.

"Can I just get the bottle, man?" I ask Anders. "It's for Aspyn. She's having a shit day."

When he consents, I take a carafe of OJ and an entire bottle of champagne back to Beck's table, and she beams brightly at me, which is worth the price of admission. Pouring her a mimosa with about 80% alcohol, I pass it to her, and Beck thanks me with a smile that sends a jolt through me.

Breakfast is served moments later, and I'm surprised when

I see Beck, Ms. Animal Fat is Bad, grab a piece of bacon and crunch on it.

"You're eating bacon?" I can't help but question her.

"Well, yeah. Who do you think obsessed about my weight and my dress size for the last ten years? It wasn't me. Eventually, I ended up giving up my favorite foods, so Sean wouldn't have a hissy fit in public about what I ordered. I've always loved bacon." She reaches for another piece, and I want to find Sean and punch him in his other fucking eye.

"I hate him," Marissa says with her eyes narrow, and lips scrunched up with anger. "I can't believe he tried to control what you ate! And I can't believe Deacon tried to control who you should fuck. Do better, boys. She's been with Sleazy Sean for ten years, and now she has all the time in the world to date around and see what kind of guy she wants to be with next. All I'm saying is, don't interfere."

I feel sufficiently lectured. "I think that's enough goading about Beck's sex life or lack of. We've established she's an adult who can make her own decisions. I wasn't trying to rain on her parade."

"Sure, buddy." Emmett rolls his eyes as if to say, *believe whatever you want, man.*

"It's okay," Beck insists. "Today, I realize I was wearing Beer Goggles last night, so we'll just leave it in the past and move on. Shall we, everyone? Please?"

"Fine." Emmett shrugs as everyone murmurs their agreement, and we dig into the delicious spread of food in front of us. I'm not much of a morning eater, but the French toast is decadent, so I can't help but shovel it into my mouth.

Beck stays as briefly as she can, eating just enough break-fast to be polite before she announces, "I've got to get the hell out of here before people finish eating and come offer me their pity. I can see everyone staring already." She darts her eyes around the room, and yeah, she's got a point. Even Tara looks sad as she makes eye contact with Beck and gives her a little wave.

"I can take you home, if you want," I volunteer.

"Thanks, but I have my Durango. I'll be fine."

"Call me if Sean gives you any trouble," I tell her, standing up and taking her hand in mine. Beck waves to everyone with her other hand, and then we walk out to her Durango with her luggage.

Beck turns to me and says, "You didn't have to push my suitcase or walk me out. And stop staring at me like I'm going to break at any time."

Maybe I know her better than she knows herself, because she's going to go home to the place she won't share with Sean for much longer, and then she's going to lose her mind. It might not happen right away, but eventually, I'll be ready to be there when she finally cracks open and lets out all the grief she's trying not to let consume her.

I hoist the bag into her backseat, slam the door, and open her driver's side door with a flourish. "Your chariot awaits, milady," I announce exaggeratedly.

"Thank you, kind sir." Aspyn always plays along. That's part of her charm. And she laughs at my awful accents.

"When the house gets too quiet, call me. I'll come by." I take her face in my hands, cupping each cheek with my palm, and I peer into her hazel eyes that look bright green in this light. Then, I kiss her forehead. "Focus on how much better life is going to get after this. Without Sean as your ball and chain, dragging you down, you can do anything you want. The future is limitless, waiting for you to make your move."

She stares at me with eyes that hold doubt and fear. I stroke her cheek with my thumb.

"It's true, Beck. There are far better things ahead of you than what you just left behind. I promise."

Finally, I see hope re-emerge in her bright eyes, and I give as charming a smile as I can conjure. "Keep in touch, Beck."

"Of course. You're my bestie." Aspyn steps into my embrace and lets me hold her tight, my hand on the back of her head as she sways against me. I hear her sniffle, but she ducks her head, gets into the car, and slams the door behind her. She doesn't look at me again, just puts her hand up over her shoulder and waves at me as she drives off.

Marissa and Bear wheel their suitcases out to the parking lot just as I'm heading back in. I give Marissa a quick hug and say our goodbyes.

Soon enough, I leave too, winding my truck down the familiar streets that lead me home.

Home is a two-story Cape Cod with an additional two thousand feet added on, and it's far bigger than what I need. When I bought it and subsequently hired the construction crew, I imagined a life of marriage, babies, and little feet running around the house and the yard. It's my biggest dream. Not that it's materialized yet, given my inability to commit for very long. I'm not a cheater; I just feel that itchy moment about three months in, where it's not fun anymore, and conversation topics run dry.

And I'd rather just hang out with Beck. That, of course, usually becomes a problem in my relationships—explaining Aspyn. The anger women justifiably feel about being second. But as long as I'm friends with Beck, she'll always have my first-place blue ribbon.

I turn on my video game console and waste the rest of Sunday getting my ass handed to me by tweens around America with potty mouths. I think some prepubescent boy just called me a 'taint.' What on Earth?

My thoughts about Beck are rapid fire, wondering what she's doing. How she's doing. If she's packing. Will she need help moving? Will she move back to her parents' house? What's next?

The doorbell rings around five, and I jump up to grab it in my flannel pants and bare chest. Beck stands there, hands in her pockets, with red-rimmed eyes.

"What's going on?" I pull her into the house.

"Fuckface is at the apartment packing his stuff, taking his sweet ass time," Beck tells me as she sighs and rubs her eyes. "Don't worry, he didn't catch me crying. As soon as I saw him on the Ring camera, I put my sunglasses on and acted like I was just about to leave, anyway. Don't want him thinking I'm sitting home alone on a perfectly good Sunday."

"Good, then don't. You can sit on my couch and cry if you need to." I wrap my arms around Beck, and she briefly lets me hold her before she shrugs me off and jumps onto my couch, pulling her knees up to her chin.

"I've got old episodes of Project Runway on the DVR. We could just numb our minds for a while. Or I can make you some dinner while you watch? I've got a frozen teriyaki chicken with stir-fry vegetables that would reheat fast enough."

"Not hungry." Beck's face is drained of color, and she nibbles her lower lip as her eyes move from mine to the paused video game on the TV screen. She doesn't respond regarding the TV show, so I flip to my DVR and pull her to my side, begging my thoughts about how beautiful she looks to go away.

I spread a blanket out over both of us, and we spent the next three hours half-comatose, killing our brain cells by binge-watching Project Runway. I'm not judging, but I hate when Beck is devoid of life like this. She's usually such a big personality, so bright, boisterous. Today, she's a zombie.

I take her feet in my hands and give her a foot rub before the pizza I finally ordered out of pure starvation arrives. Beck leans her head forward and rests it on my shoulder as I move my hands up her sculpted calves and then tickle the back of her knee. She smiles just wide enough that I'm glad I took the chance, but I back off and return to her feet as she makes little groans when I dig into the sore spots. I can imagine some other fun ways to make her moan, but I tell my inner dude to shut up. Today is about giving Beck what she needs, not my hormones.

After we scarf pizza, Beck stands up and sighs. "I'd better go. Thanks for tolerating my company. I know I'm not the most fun right now."

I'd tell her I more than tolerate her, but she's already walking out and jumping into her Durango. All I can do is wave as she squeals her tires out of my driveway and races down my street.

She's not herself, and it kills me.

ASPYN

Three days without more than a couple of hours of sleep has me losing my mind. Despite what a buffoon my ex is, I miss having another warm body in the house. I jump when the refrigerator makes ice in the middle of the night, and I startle at all the strange noises whose incidence seems to increase when there's no one else around. It is too quiet. Maybe I can get a dog, since Sean never let me before.

I do all the things I love: taking long baths with a glass of wine, dancing in my kitchen to my favorite songs, going for long runs outside, and reading a sexy romance book. But despite everything, I still feel alone. *Am* alone. I miss work and my clients, but everyone needs some time to heal. I told my workplace I had COVID, which bought me five days off work, exactly the period I have allowed myself to mourn my demolished relationship.

I wander aimlessly around the house, occasionally throwing things into a box or two I'd pulled out of the garage. My parents' house is furnished, but my bedroom there has remained unchanged since I was fifteen, when I redecorated it with pink and white everywhere. Now I mostly detest pink for décor, opting instead for neutrals and splashes of turquoise and blue, and decorating with macramé, ocean scenes, and photos of our friends and family.

Except...there is no "our" anymore, and the photos hurt to look at. I removed all the ones with Sean in them and moved a smiling photo of Tara, Deacon, and me to the bedside table. We'd had it taken at a roller rink, where my ass spent more time on the ground than on the skates, but I'd still had an amazing time.

Deacon texts every day, and I've replied a few times, but mostly keep to myself. Grief is an ugly thing, and I don't want to feel on display for anyone. There are some high points, though. Sean was gone by the time I got home from Deacon's last week, so at least I hadn't been forced to run into him again. Most of his personal effects are gone, along with his mountain of scrubs from the closet, which has been one slight relief. Not having to clean up after him has also been nice.

I sit on the sofa in pink fuzzy socks, scrolling through my texts, my phone buzzing in my hand with beautiful beach photos from Tara's honeymoon. Then, Deacon texts, asking if I want to get out of the house. Seconds later, Marissa messages to apologize if it came off that she was "pushing me at the bartender" and promises to be my cheerleader whenever I'm ready to move on.

As I doze off a short time later, I hear the doorbell chime. Sighing, I bang my shin on the paddle-board coffee table I intend to take with me to my parents' place and throw the door open.

"You don't call, you don't write..." Deacon stands there, one hand on his hip, the other holding up a bag of greasy fried chicken from our favorite local place. "I don't know if you're eating and can't let you waste away. I can come in with the chicken, or you can just take it and promise me you'll eat."

A smile pulls at my lips as I reach for the bag, whip around, and call over my shoulder, "I hope you remembered the biscuits."

"Doll face, after ten years, I've learned a few things about you. How could I ever forget your obsession with biscuits? I ordered a half dozen, so you can have as many as you want." Deacon reaches into the cupboard for plates while I retrieve forks and knives. We spread our food out on the kitchen table.

I sit down with a huff. "I'm sorry I haven't been answering all of your texts. I haven't really felt up to talking to anyone." I gesture to the food. "So, thanks for this."

Deacon's gaze softens as his ocean-blue eyes stare back into my hazel ones. He holds eye contact tenderly and then reaches across the table to put his hand over mine. "Hey. You're grieving. I get that. I needed to see you and make sure you're okay."

"Yeah, I'll be okay eventually." My voice is determined. "I won't let that man ruin my life. Unfortunately, I'm not sleeping well alone, constantly spooked by noises that were normal a week ago. So weird."

"Let me take the couch tonight, see if it helps. I have my gym bag in the trunk with clean clothes in it, and I don't mind."

"You gonna protect me from the refrigerator making ice?" I laugh, peeling off the crispy skin on a piece of chicken and shoving it into my mouth, closing my eyes in enjoyment.

"If the need arises."

We eat in companionable silence, and then I grasp my full belly and let out a deep breath. "Thanks, Deac. I needed this."

"Sure, Beck. I'm either going to force you into a shower or out of the house. It's a nice day out. We could do some fishing."

Sean hated fishing. He refused to touch the worms, so I had to bait his hooks. He was exposed to bodily fluids and blood daily, which seemed far worse than worms, so his avoidance annoyed me a little extra. I roll my eyes in remembrance.

"Yeah, let's do that. I won't have to bait your hooks, will I?"

"I'm not Sean."

I change from my PJs into a pair of beat-up cargo pants and an old Alanis Morissette concert t-shirt. Her song "You Oughtta Know" has been just the song I've needed to get through the week, so I turn it up loud in Deacon's Jeep.

I can't help but smile as Deacon sings along in perfect pitch. We shout out the lyrics together, drawing a few strange looks from people stopped beside us at traffic lights.

After a quick stop for bait, we arrive at our favorite fishing spot. It's such a gorgeous September day that people are everywhere at the lake, so we walk a distance to find an empty public dock and set up our camp chairs. Everything about nature is so healing and being at our favorite spot soothes my soul.

Within five minutes, I reel in a bluegill. Deacon insists on taking a photo of me holding my prize, but I quickly release it back to its home. I guess, in a way, I can relate to the fish. Having been on someone's hook and thrown back out into the wild. Sean was nothing more than a hook with some attractive bait who had reeled me in and savagely kept me when he should've let me go a long time ago.

I feel Deacon's hand on the small of my back as I stand, staring into the water in a daze.

"Hey. It's going to be okay." His soft words touch me, and

all I can do is turn and press my face into Deacon's shoulder, nodding against his soft shirt as I hold my pole out to the side to avoid hitting him with it. I catch a glimpse of the ring he'd given me that I hadn't taken off yet and breathe in his scent—a mix of nutty soap, hints of lavender from his laundry detergent, and a woodsy smell all his own. I couldn't remember the last time I'd been in his arms this long, though, as he usually kept a respectful distance in front of Sean.

"I like it here," I whisper.

"It's a pretty little lake." Deacon holds me tighter with one arm encircling me.

"Your arms, I mean." My face flushes.

He holds up one finger as if to say, "One second," sets his pole down carefully, freeing up his second arm to give me a giant bear hug that instantaneously makes me feel safe and relaxed. Better than I'd felt in many days. Deacon gives the best hugs; he's practically a human teddy bear.

Bright sun breaks through the clouds and shines down on the lake, the gentle waves appearing to shimmer in its rays. The water is so clear and blue and inviting, it begs to be jumped into, but it's not warm enough. The time for swimming has come and gone already, especially since I hadn't packed any towels or blankets.

When we sit down, I wipe a stray tear as Deacon says, "I heard from Sean."

My throat dries up at the thought, and I squeeze my eyes shut. "What—what did he have to say?"

"Bullshit excuses I saw right through. An appeal to my emotions, to our history, trying to convince me to be loyal to him. Tried to turn me against you, like that would ever work."

"Sounds like him. Sean can be convincing. He turns it around on you and makes you feel like you're crazy until you almost believe you are." I shake my head, wondering why I'd stayed so long with someone who made me feel batshit insane half the time.

"Yeah, he's got that down. I made it simple for him and told him I chose you. The only way he would ever have my friendship again is if he did some serious work on himself. Which I think we both know he won't do." Deacon sighs loudly as my phone buzzes.

I try to ignore the text message, but once I see it's from Tara, I peek at it.

Dear fucking Christ.

The words crawl off the screen and burrow themselves in my belly, twisting up my guts, making me feel physically ill.

Shivers shoot down my spine and back up again as I read.

"Sean got his nurse pregnant. You deserve to know. I'm so sorry."

I silently hand the phone to Deacon and lean over the water as the food we just ate not an hour earlier comes back up. Fuck, I hate spilling my literal guts into the clear water. Deacon hands me a bottle of water and a fast-food napkin to clean up, but my stomach keeps twisting while I swish. I collapse to my knees, hot tears streaming down my cheeks.

Strong arms pull me up to standing and surround me, and I bathe Deacon's shoulder with my salty tears. Sean is going to be a father, leaving me single and alone at twenty-nine, longing for children of my own but starting over from zero.

"Better her than you," Deacon declares as he holds me. "She's stuck with him for the rest of her life because they'll share a child. You can find a good man this time and fall in love and have babies with someone who won't cheat on you. I know it sucks, but it's a blessing. It's an opportunity disguised as a painful ending."

"It's really heavily disguised." My voice shakes.

"Do you want to get out of here?" Deacon reaches down to squeeze my hand, and I whisper that I want to relax for a few minutes, let the lake air settle my stomach.

I settle back into my camp chair and cast out into the water again. My heart twinges with the recollection of my father teaching me to fish at age five; my very first catch had been a bluegill. Now, he's thousands of miles away, with no idea yet that the man he trusted to take care of me had betrayed me.

That's one thing I still need to do: tell my parents about Sean and take their house off the Airbnb site. Their house is further up in the mountains than I'm used to in my tiny Colorado Springs suburb, with an incredible view of Pike's Peak. It will mean a longer drive to work.

Deacon's pole bends, and he reels in a lovely rainbow trout. I smile brightly and make a big deal of taking a photo of him with it, until I point at the water and demand he toss her back in.

"Alright, fine." He unhooks the gorgeous fish and lets it splash back into the water. "Just for you, Beck. I cook a mean trout."

"I love trout. I can eat it if I don't see its eyes first. Once I've seen it alive, forget about it."

"That's an odd stance for a fisherwoman." Deacon winks at me and gives me a serene smile that affects me like it's contagious. I return his grin and tell Deacon, "Well, I love surprising you."

Deacon moves his camp chair closer and rests his free hand on my knee, and I breathe deeply, appreciative of his warm, reassuring touch. In the quiet moments, we sit fishing together, and peace returns to my soul; somehow, I know I am going to survive this.

Late that night, after a long game of Scrabble and a ton of spicy wings, I tell Deacon I don't need him to stay over. I'm feeling so much better that I can give this alone thing a shot. He reluctantly grabs his things and heads home while I curl up in the bed I once shared with Sean. The bed I'd picked out and paid for, and sure as hell had no intention of leaving for him.

Glancing around in the dark at all the furniture, I ruminate about how I'm going to need a U-Haul, and by the time my brain lets me stop focusing on that, it's nearly 5 a.m. My eyes are wide open but bleary, and I pray for sleep to take me in its embrace and put an end to my obsessing.

Without a second thought, I wrestle up the loose floorboard under my side of the bed, where I've been known to keep items Sean wouldn't have appreciated. I find the baggie that houses exactly two pre-rolled joints a friend from work had given me when her husband opened his vape shop several months ago.

Then, I search for a match, but the ones I scrounge up from under the sink are all soggy. After trying to burn several, I finally find one that lights up the end of the joint, and I sit in bed, quietly smoking pot in total peace. No paranoid Sean staying two rooms away for fear that he might inhale and fail a random drug test that he's only done once in the entire time he's worked at the hospital. I no longer give a shit as I blow smoke from my lungs into the bedroom I won't call mine for much longer, no longer caring about the stench and the way it may cling to the expensive curtains.

"Fuck you, Sean," I say aloud between drags, tilting my head back and taking a puff, then exhaling out my nose and mouth slowly, the smoke headed for the ceiling. My body calms immediately, but I know I shouldn't finish this whole thing by myself, so I carefully put it out with the base of a vase. I turn the vase on its side and let the joint rest on the glass to cool off, not wanting to start the whole place on fire. Correction: trying hard *not* to want to set the house on fire to leave Sean with nothing but ashes.

No. That's not me. I'm not an arsonist, nor am I malicious, but I've had my fill of being wronged and feel myself falling into a stoic bitterness about it. So, I defy Sean in every way possible as I take my time packing up the house in the next couple of days.

I bring my too-large vibrator out to the couch and masturbate in the bright daylight on his favorite recliner, without a towel beneath me.

I put together a tray full of deviled eggs, the smell of which Sean had hated, and happily ate them over the course of three days.

Smoked the rest of the joint the next night to help me fall asleep at a decent hour without overthinking everything.

I slip the promise ring he'd given me, a tiny pearl flanked by lab-created diamonds, into the loose floorboard. When I leave, I'll tell him it's "in the house somewhere" if he wants to re-gift it to his slutty nurse with his fake promises.

Then, for breakfast on my fourth day home from work, I uncap his most expensive bourbon and wash my pancakes down with it. I'm living and loving my Goodbye Sean Tour when the bell rings around noon, and I walk to the door with joint number two hanging out of my mouth.

"Well, if it isn't my bestie, the degenerate," Deacon tuts as I throw the door open. All I can do in response is giggle, because, well, this is good weed. What can I say? It's medicinal.

He plucks the joint from my fingers, shuts the door behind him, takes a long hit, then coughs until I have no choice but to laugh at him.

"Lightweight." I elbow him.

"Hey, you better be nice. I brought tacos, and you look like you're wasting away." Deacon rolls his eyes, holds up the bag that smells like absolute heaven, brings it to the kitchen, and pulls out a couple of paper plates as he hits the joint again and hands it back to me.

I inhale deeply and sigh the smoke back out.

"Can I put this out now, or do you want it?" I ask him as I open the fridge and select two Dr. Peppers, then slide in beside him at the kitchen island. Sean hates when we eat here, getting food on his pristine white marble, so that makes this even more fun.

"Might as well finish it," I reason with a naughty giggle.

❦ 10 ❦

DEACON

"**A**nd you called me a lightweight!" I proclaim, laughing until my eyes fill with tears. We're both on the floor watching stand-up comedy, giggling endlessly, and engaging in some pretend wrestling that quickly becomes a tickle fight. Beck is running from me, hiding behind objects that are far too small to cover her up, and I'm pretending I can't see her.

Now we're playing a game of hot-cold, and as I wander closer to Beck hiding behind a recliner, she yells, "Hot! So hot, you're on fire!" I turn away intentionally, and she slips behind the other couch while she shouts, "Brr! You're in Siberia!"

"When I find you, I am going to tickle you," I announce, putting my hands over my eyes and hearing her slip into the first-floor primary bedroom. Apparently, we've moved on to Hide and Seek.

"I'll huff and puff and..." I wheeze from inhaling too much weed. "Something or other that goes after that in the kids' book?" Quietly, I squeeze through the door and see a Beck-sized lump beneath the blankets of her bed.

I jump on top of her without giving her my full weight, and I find her sides through the blanket and dig my fingertips in, tickling her until she cries, "Uncle! Uncle!"

When I flip the blanket down, Beck's got tears streaming down her red face, and she holds up her pointer finger with feigned seriousness. "No more! No more or I'll pee my pants! And you're supposed to blow my house down, but instead, all you did was huff and puff."

Beck stands and starts walking sideways to the bathroom, but I don't ask questions. I curl up on the bed while she uses the bathroom, and then she emerges from her ex's closet with a pair of his swimming trunks.

"How about we go sit in my ex's hot tub out back?" Beck gives a shoulder shimmy. She taps her chin like she's deep in thought. "Wait, did I already ask you if you wanted to get in the hot tub? Why am I the one deep in thought?"

I tap my chin, or at least I think it's my chin, but it could be my jaw, who knows? I'm stoned out of my mind, and at this point, I have to wonder if one of us could manage to drown in the four-foot hot tub.

"Fine." I pluck the swimming trunks out of her hands and glance at the size. They're a little snug when I put them on, and when Beck sees me, her eyes widen, and her mouth falls open.

"What?" I demand.

"Well, I can sort of see the outline of your dick?"

"And you couldn't keep a shirt on around me at the wedding, so now we're even. Come on, let's go." I roll my eyes.

Pushing open the back door, each of us slinging a towel over one shoulder, Beck tries her best to open the top of the hot tub. Eventually, I help her, but she doesn't notice my hand, so she declares that she's Shera (whoever that is) and falls into the bubbling water with a splash.

It's chilly today, the perfect temperature for this, so I follow her in and sink onto the ledge, the water covering me up to my collarbone. Beck is still going on and on about how strong she is, and she flexes her biceps to prove it before she leans in and kisses each one—they're pretty impressive.

Beck giggles uproariously as she sits down beside me. "Or maybe She-Man? I dunno, but it feels great to laugh like this. I can't remember the last time I felt this light. Must have been all that tickling."

"Definitely not all the weed." I raise my eyebrow.

"Maybe finishing it wasn't the greatest idea we've ever had." Beck tilts her head from side to side. "The whole world is moving."

"That's because you're moving your head," I point out, but she insists, and I don't put up an argument. When she immediately starts singing the old-school bologna brand theme song of our youth, she misspells "Oscar" as "*Ocsar*," and I jump in to correct her. She takes a break just to argue with me, so I join in and sing it her decidedly wrong way.

"New song!" Beck launches into REO Speedwagon's "Keep on Loving You." She stands up in the water and sings passionately into an invisible microphone, really shouting the lyrics out, though I'm confused over her song choice.

I fully expected a little "Shake It Off" by her lord and savior, Taylor Swift, but I don't mind. I try singing along with her off-key voice, but she keeps holding the notes too long—it's still adorable. When Beck's not expecting it, I tickle her sides in her pink bikini and fight the urge to untie her top. This medicinal shit has lowered my inhibitions. Beck falls into my arms, giggling, and then curls up in my lap. Her giggles run dry, and she rests her face against my shoulder.

I've spent ten years wondering how she would feel in my arms like this, and I know this isn't the right moment. Beck's high as a kite and grieving the loss of a long-term relationship, so I cradle her there and start to sing, "Shake It Off," albeit reluctantly.

Beck's face lights up. She stands back up and starts shaking her hips as she joins in. She's never looked more beautiful than she does right now, in the fading daylight with rose-and-violet decorated skies behind her. The Rockies stand tall in the background as she sings. I want to do something stupid, like yank her into me and see how her lips taste, but that's not what she needs right now.

Eventually, we both turn so pruney that we stumble out of the hot tub. The day has turned into night, the waning gibbous moon bright overhead, and we stop to look up in the backyard for a few minutes. Beck puts her hands up in the air and spins in the grass, perhaps worshiping the moon. I don't ask her to qualify her behavior.

Her body shudders with shivers as she runs into the house, and when I follow her, I hear the shower running in the primary bathroom. My towel is soaked, so I tap on the door and ask if I can come grab a fresh towel.

"Of course," Beck yells a little too loudly.

When I open the door, I don't mean to look at her naked body behind the plain glass door, beneath the rain shower head. But damn myself, I do. Then, I stare a second too long, the sight of her stunning me into silence. Now my mind's blank and the towel I came in here for is completely forgotten, replaced with the vision of her wet body glistening in the shower just feet away from mine.

She's got her back to me, her round, tight ass on display for a moment before the shower's steam conceals it, and I gulp, my dick hardening in these stupid, too-tight trunks. Shaking my head as if to clear it, I finally grab a towel and flee, closing the door behind me to give Beck some privacy—because apparently, I'm a pervy guy who can't turn away from his best friend's incredible ass.

I dress quickly, feeling stone-cold sober now. When I'm about to walk out the front door, Beck, clad only in a purple robe, calls out and asks me where I'm going. Water clings to her skin, and I long to lick the droplets away and taste her, and that's why I need to go.

"Got a couple of things I still need to accomplish at home," I lie.

"Oh." Her face falls. "Okay. Well, thanks for the fun day. I really needed it."

And I need to go home and take the coldest shower known to man.

"You're welcome. You all good?" I bite my lip, angling my body away from Beck so she can't see my tented jeans.

"All good." Beck nods. "Go do what you gotta do. See you soon."

Beck turns and walks back toward her bedroom, and I take the moment to escape.

Except all I feel is shame as I walk to my Jeep and climb in. What Beck needs is a friend, not a horny guy who lingers too long in the bathroom to glimpse the incredible view of her backside. Not a guy who hoped fervently she'd turn, so he'd get an eyeful of her amazing breasts—though it's not as if I don't have them memorized in my brain. I'd taken a mental picture when she was drunk at the wedding, and damn it, I feel as guilty about that as I do my questionable actions today.

After I drive home, I get into a cold shower and wonder how the hell I'm going to keep my eyes and hands off Aspyn Beckett until she's ready to move on.

I might die trying.

ASPYN

Tara returns from her honeymoon the next day, dragging Wendy and Marissa over to Sean's place, where I'm still living. I no longer think of it as my own, even though I've lived here for eight years. We all curl up on the couches to watch a slideshow she'd put together of photos and videos from her Caribbean trip.

We sit, drinking Prosecco, giving the standard 'oohs' and 'aahs' over the honeymoon montage.

As I watch, a text comes through from an unknown number that Sean must be using, since I'd blocked his phone from contacting me.

21 days. -Sean

I long to tell him to fuck off, but ignore the text, instead, well aware that it's been seven full days since our breakup. Twenty-one more days to move out. I hate that he's sent me a reminder that this place would be a memory soon, and I'd be settling back into my parents' house, a half hour farther from my friends, in a couple of weeks.

When the topic shifts to Sean and his baby mama, I squirm uncomfortably on the couch and deny giving a shit.

"He's moving her in here as soon as you leave," Tara says, reaching out to squeeze my hand tightly. "Sorry to be the one to tell you. I told him to lose my number for a while. Can't help but be so angry with him for the way he treated you and the bullshit he fed Cody about you being infertile. That's unforgivable. Have you heard from him?"

Fresh tears spring to my eyes. I wipe them away furiously, pissed that I have even a single tear left in me to cry over Sean. "Just long enough for him to remind me how many days he's giving me before he moves Nurse Q in."

"That makes me so mad—he's got someone lined up like the last decade meant nothing. I want to kick him in his lying, cheating dick," Marissa says, crunching a mouthful of popcorn.

"His black eye is pretty epic, though," Tara tells us with a laugh. "I mean, he deserved it. Mom sent him home as soon as she saw it, after what I heard was quite a lecture. I believe she referred to you, Aspyn, as 'the best you could possibly do.' Mama meant business."

Okay, that makes me feel moderately better. Cecile is usually kind and gentle, so to know she stood up for me to her own son gives me the warm fuzzies.

I let out a gigantic sigh, and Wendy laughs as she looks up from her phone. "Sean's already cheating on this Nurse Q. Jett just accidentally sent me a video on his phone. He's at the club with Sean, and he most definitely has his hand up some tramp's crop top." Wendy gawks at the phone with her eyebrows raised so high they nearly hit her hairline.

"Aspyn doesn't need to see that!" Marissa plucks the phone out of Wendy's hand, but I grab it out of hers so quickly, I manage to hit play on the video to see it with my own two eyes. Yep, there he is, cheating on his pregnant girl-friend, which is clear only between the flashes of the strobe lights overhead. They're practically getting it on right there on the dance floor, her circling her hips back against Sean's dark jeans, the expensive pair I got him for his birthday.

"Gross," I say, but it's kind of like a train wreck I don't want to look away from. It's only a twenty-second video, but it's such a good example of the person Sean Wright really is. Grinding with a random girl who looks about a decade too young for him, while his knocked-up Nurse Q probably sits at home waiting for him, like I had done so many of the past 3,650 days.

Nah. No more.

I hand Wendy back her phone with a smile. "Hey, you know the best part of this?"

Wendy arches a perfectly threaded eyebrow while Tara stares at me, as if wondering how I could possibly answer that particular question.

"It's not me he's cheating on." I press my lips together to keep from laughing, but the edges pull up too hard not to bust out an ear-to-ear grin.

Tara gives me a high five while Wendy bursts into giggles.

I jump up and run to the freezer, where I'm storing one hell of an expensive tequila. Finding champagne flutes, I pour the delicious liquid, and then I cut lime wedges for all of us, set them on a platter, and carefully carry everything back to the coffee table.

"I've seen saving this tequila for the right moment, and guess what? This is it." I hand out the drinks and bring mine up to my nose to take a whiff of it. The color has a beautiful, slightly golden hue, indicating that it was aged for a long time in oak barrels.

"Ahhh, this is the stuff. First, we aerate it by just giving it a gentle swish. Then, we smell." I demonstrate, and my friends follow along.

We all sniff the tequila, me for the second time. I get notes of citrus and a hint of floral aroma. "Okay, then we should cheer to..." I pause, trying to think.

"Fuckboy exes being long gone?" Wendy suggests.

"Freedom?" Tara adds, raising her glass high.

"Fucking new people!" Marissa sounds too excited.

"Friendship, too." A smile tugs at my lips as I clink my glass against theirs, and we all call out, "Cheers!"

I take a tentative sip, and the flavor hits me right in the throat. I swirl it around my mouth for a few seconds and swallow, the citrus notes singing in the aftertaste. This is the good shit. I repeat the process until I grab the tequila bottle and pour us another.

"I guess this makes tonight a sleepover," Marissa decides as she takes the champagne flute and swirls the golden liquid.

"No problem. That's why we have a sleeper sofa. Well, that's why I do. Sean will arrive home to no couch at all, just his precious recliner. Oh, and I got high the other day and masturbated all over the expensive suede." I let out a cackle and add, "Maybe just avoid the chair tonight."

All my friends tilt their heads back and laugh until we're all sniffling and tearing up, and we finally steel ourselves so we can enjoy our second glass of tequila.

"To vibrators, our trusty companions," Marissa announces with a snort, and all four of us clink our glasses to that one and fall into a comfortable silence.

"It just sucks that I can't hold all his shit against him given that Sean's my brother. Wish I could give him back, but we're thirty years too late for that." Tara groans.

I sense that this is troubling Tara more than she wants to admit. "Listen, girl. I don't need you to hate him for me. I have enough hate for him on my own. You have to give Nurse

Q a chance and love this baby regardless of how you feel about Sean's despicable actions. He's not a good guy, but he's still your family. I can get away, but you're stuck. Take a few weeks to give him the cold shoulder and then start putting up with his miserable ass again. That's all you can do."

Tara throws her arms around me, nearly tackling me. "Thank you for understanding. I want you in my life forever, but I can't keep Sean out of mine either."

"I can," Marissa decides. "Bear isn't a big fan of his right now either. I think he's decidedly Team Aspyn."

"Cody, too," Tara admits. "He keeps asking about you, girl."

"I'm stuck with Sean." Wendy heaves a sigh. "With Jett being his cousin and all. Yuck. We'll be family one day." She spits out "family" like it's a dirty word, and she wants to use mouthwash after saying it.

"If Jett ever gets off his lazy ass and proposes. You're twenty-eight now, right, Wendy? What's taking him so long?" Marissa asks.

Wendy's jet-black hair falls into her face as she shakes her head. Her ice blue eyes shine with tears as Marissa clearly hits a delicate subject with all the grace of a fucking freight train.

I close my eyes for a second, hating the look on Wendy's face. When she croaks out, "I don't know," I throw my arms around her and tell her, "He's not stupid, Wen. He'll put a ring on your finger. He's not Sean, I promise."

She holds me tight and whispers, "Thank you."

As she vents about six years without a ring, I pull up a quick text to Jett and write, "Don't be a dick like Sean. Go to the goddamn jeweler and pick something out. Soon."

When he replies with, "On it, but shut up about it," I try not to smile.

I do, however, open my mouth to say, "I bet you it'll happen anytime. Let's just say I have a really good feeling about it. He's got a good head on his shoulders, and he's not stupid enough to lose you, Wendy."

She gives me a winning grin. "If you're so sure, I'll choose to believe you. My mom keeps telling me that cliché line about not buying the cow when he gets the milk for free, and she warns me that moving in with him last year was a mistake because now he gets me to be his domestic goddess with a bare ring finger."

"Your mother, bless her heart, is one of the most pessimistic people I've ever met," Tara tells her. "Now, come on. How about one more shot?"

"Only if you want me to fall unconscious," I mutter. The alcohol has warmed my body, brought heat to my cheeks, and the room feels like it's closing in on me. "Be back." I slip out to the backyard and admire my gorgeous view of the Rockies, thinking for a brief second how much I'll miss this view.

I tug my phone out of my pocket and take a photo of the dazzling stars above, beside a bright moon and Venus. Sean had never been much for stargazing, but I adore how insignificant I feel in the grand scheme of things when I look up. So small—yet some astrophysicists would say created from stardust itself. Me—the tiniest blip in the universe but containing the universe within me. I sigh with the wonder of it all, and I wish, in this moment, Deacon were at my side. Something tells me he would appreciate my inner musings.

When I turn to go back inside, I'm carrying more peace with me than before.

The girls are pulling out the couch and making the bed with sheets they know I keep in the hall closet, while Marissa, known for her ability to sleep anywhere at any time, just curls up on the other, much softer, sofa and closes her eyes.

"Bedtime?" I ask, locking the sliding glass door behind me and turning off the oppressive kitchen light.

"Yes. Love you," Marissa tells me as she turns away from

the TV light, and then gets so quiet, I'm sure she's already asleep.

I venture into the living room and perch on the recliner as Tara selects Jimmy Kimmel from the DVR. Minutes later, we all fall asleep, bellies full of Prosecco and tequila, hearts full of friendship none of us would sacrifice for anything.

12

DEACON

I spend a good chunk of Saturday morning in the gym with Cody, who claims he ate so much on their honeymoon, he gained six pounds. He insists he needs someone to spot him on the weight benches, and while I despise the inside of a gym, I agree because he's one of my bros.

"So, you and Aspyn seem close lately," Cody tells me as we move over to the stair steppers for a burst of cardio.

"We've always been. It's not new at all." *Though perhaps seeing her naked in the shower and salivating over her is a little unusual.*

"All right. Just saying, it's good that you're there for her. I think she needs you. Damn, man. What did we ever see in Sean to begin with? He's Tara's sister and now my brother-in-law, so that's pretty binding. But back when, I hung out with him when it was optional...and I mean, why? What did we ever see in him? He's a womanizing piece of trash."

I harumph in agreement as I start the stair stepper. "He wasn't always like this. He was a lonely, insecure high schooler when we met, desperate to be cool enough to have friends. I got him into ball, climbing, and hiking, but he was always a little prissy. Then, by college, he turned on a false sense of bravado and learned to hone his charm. That's the thing. He can charm anyone, but it's all an act. The goodness I saw in him early in our friendship is long gone."

"All he ever does is talk about how cool he is. Maybe over-compensating because he knows he's a loser." Cody goes hard on the stair stepper, so our conversation ends there.

We grab smoothies from the shop next door before I climb in my truck and head home, Beck on my mind. I heard from Jett that she'd had a sleepover last night with her girls, and I hoped they were able to boost her mood and show her a good time.

Jett had shown me a video of Sean being a filthy asshole on the dance floor last night, his hands up the shirt of some twenty-one-year-old, which had disgusted me. Not that I thought he wouldn't cheat on Nurse Q despite her being pregnant with his child, because I know Sean is motivated mostly by a challenge. Once he's gotten a woman, he bores easily, and it's all about the next thrill. It's so clear to me now, I wonder how I hadn't seen it more easily over the last years of his relationship with Beck.

I'd saved Sean's ass one too many times and fed him sweet lines to say to Beck. Showed up at restaurants when he was about to stand her up. Reminded him how good he had it with Beck. The watch from last Christmas is a prime example.

I'm already pointing my truck in the direction of Beck's house instead of mine, under the guise of dropping off boxes I'd gotten from a neighbor. When I ring the bell, she throws the door open wearing a purple crop top that shows off her flat stomach and big, wide-legged gray sweatpants that she has rolled up at the bottom. Her light gold hair sits atop her head in a messy knot, and she looks effortlessly perfect.

"Hey! What a surprise. Come on in." Beck stands back and opens the door with a big smile. The urge to bend and kiss her is so strong, I have to take two deep breaths and let it pass.

"How was your girls' night?" I kick off my sneakers and make my way to her fridge, where I'll snatch one of Sean's ungodly expensive electrolyte waters. It's the last one, and I gulp it all down.

Beck gives a light laugh. "Sean will miss all the water that I've been drinking. I had a great night with the girls. Way too much tequila, though. I've taken like four Ibuprofen this morning, trying to combat my headache. Thankfully, it's cloudy and dreary, because the sun would hurt my eyes."

"Oof," I groan. "Did you finally get out that good tequila you've had in the freezer for ages?"

"Yep, and it was incredible. You know, after it stopped burning." Beck laughs and then beckons me to the bedroom.

"I've got a truck full of boxes," I announce as she points to the bed at an array of jewelry, candles, photos of Beck and Sean, and other odds and ends.

"And I've got a bed full of presents from Sean to take to Goodwill. It's that or burn them, but why do that when someone else can enjoy these things?"

That's when I spot it—the watch. It's rose-gold and just as perfect for Beck's slim wrist as it was the day I purchased it for her from my favorite jeweler. The watch was supposed to be her Christmas present. Sean had seen it on my counter one day and commented how lovely it was, and asked if it was for my short-term girlfriend, Cassie. When I told him it was for Aspyn, he got a sour look on his face and told me it was too expensive.

A few days later, he called me in a panic, asking if he could buy it off me to give to her as an anniversary present. A quick glance at the clock, which read 10 p.m, showed me that he'd nearly forgotten their nine-year anniversary.

"You can't give this one away." I pluck out the rose-gold watch and perch on the bed beside all her unwanted items. "This has a story you're not aware of."

So, I fill her in. Every little detail. "It was always from me, never from Sean," I finish. "So, how about I help you put it on?"

Beck's eyes are filled with unshed tears as she looks at me in wonder. "You did that for Sean?"

I look away. "Not Sean. For you. You didn't deserve to be forgotten on your anniversary. All I really cared about was that it made you happy, whether it was from that prick or me."

Beck paces in front of me for a minute before I see the tears streaming down her cheeks.

"I knew he didn't pick it out. When he gave it to me, I kept thinking how well he knew me to have bought something so perfect for me. Then, he apologized and said they were all out of gold, so he *had* to get me a rose-gold one, which is my favorite anyway. I hadn't heard a word from him all day, and then he shows up with this perfect watch at 11:09 p.m.? Yeah, I remember the time, because I'd been waiting on him all day. It seemed too convenient."

I watch Beck sniffle back her angry tears, and she suddenly turns to me, throwing her arms around me. "I didn't know how I was going to part with the amazing watch. Thank you for telling me the truth about it, Deac. Now, I'll keep it and wear it proudly, with full awareness of who knows me well enough to have purchased it for me. Thank you."

My arms encircle her, but Beck tosses herself against me, making me tip over. She's on top of me now, her chest pressed to mine with our legs hanging off the bed as she snuggles into my neck and sighs. I don't mind the feel of her salty, wet tears on me, nor the feeling of her heart hammering in her chest through my own skin.

"Of course it was you," Beck whispers, inches from my ear. She presses her forehead to my cheek and reaches up to cup my other cheek with her palm. "You're the best of men, Deacon Ambrose. You give me hope that not every guy is a selfish man whore."

I should tell her how I feel, like my mother had begged me to do from her deathbed, but she's less than one week out of the biggest breakup of her life.

So, all I do is whisper, "You deserve the world, Beck. You won't settle again."

She sniffles and slides off to my side, pressing her head to my shoulder as she exhales noisily. "Living my life the way I want is my priority now, rather than replacing him with version 2.0. It feels so good to do exactly what I want, when I want to. Eat what I want—smoke when I want, without him overreacting about it and going on and on about the expensive drapes. Using a vibrator that's bigger than him, when he was so insecure, I had to keep it hidden. Ugh, I mean, I hope I won't always be alone, but even that would be preferable to ending up with someone like Sean. Did you see the video Jett took of him with his fingers on the nipples of a girl that couldn't be older than college-aged?"

She sits up, and I follow her lead. "Yes, I had that distinct pleasure this morning. Gag me, right?"

"Nurse Q at home waiting for him, and he still feels the need to pinch the nips of some hot coed?" Beck sends the most massive eye roll up at the ceiling. "Give me a fucking break. But it hit me last night. Yeah, he may be cheating, but at least it's not on me."

Beck shimmies a little, which makes me burst out laughing.

"No, it's not."

"Small favors. I couldn't be more overjoyed about that," Beck adds, doing a pirouette with a bright smile, making her look downright sunny, despite the tears she'd just cried. "By the way, I have pulled pork in the slow cooker. Do you smell it? It smells so good. Sean hated it when I ate pork."

Man, Sean was a dick. How had it taken me so long to see it? Why had I made excuses over the years for him? A long history with someone is no reason to give them the benefit of the doubt instead of facing the cold, hard reality that they're essentially a goblin from the depths of hell.

"Why are you smirking?" Beck asks, pinching my cheeks and staring up at me.

"Just picturing Sean as some Godzilla-like character rising from hell itself." I chuckle as she roars with laughter.

"Love that stunning visual." Beck sighs, and it sounds happy. "Anyway, do you want to bring in some boxes? I have piles everywhere but ran out of boxes yesterday."

I do her bidding, which means building the boxes with clear packing tape and stuffing packing peanuts around all her breakable prized possessions, including the entire set of purple ceramic plates she'd purchased when she moved in.

Beck's all about revenge, and I love it. She's leaving Sean one solitary plate—a prank gift from some Christmas long ago. It's plastic with a picture of a cock on the front. Not the male variety, though that would have been funny, but of a male chicken. I half-expect her to leave a Post-it on it with the words, "Oh, look, it's you." But she lets the plate make the proper statement.

Beck brings me a big box. "I know I said a few days ago that I'm He-Man, but could you lift the espresso machine down into this box?"

I laugh at her audacity. "You're taking it, huh? He's going to miss that."

"It was a gift from my parents. To Sean, but that's a technicality. I think they'd want me to have it, given what a schmuck he was the whole time we dated." Beck beams. "And then in this box, could you pretty please, oh-so-carefully, pack my blender?"

Snorting, I shake my head. "You mean that nine-hundred-dollar monstrosity Sean uses to make his workout shake every morning?"

Beck's eyes light up. "I imagine him walking back in here and seeing it's missing. Maybe he'll shed a tear. Maybe he'll curse my name. Who know? I imagine he'll try to text me, but by then, I'll have blocked his number. He can buy his own monstrosity. This one's mine, and it was meant for margaritas, not kale, spinach, and blueberries." Beck shudders at the thought.

I press my hand to the small of her back and inch her closer to me. "You, Beck, are incredible. Your propensity for spite is so gloriously unexpected and unhinged, I'm impressed, terrified, and hell, maybe a little turned on."

I wink at her as she bites her bottom lip exaggeratedly and whispers, "You ain't seen nothing yet, baby."

Despite my full knowledge that she's joking, I love the way "baby" sounds directed at me from those luscious, full, dusky-pink lips of hers.

"Show me more, show me more," I demand lowly, leaning into her like she's mesmerizing me. Our gazes lock, and she smiles slowly.

"If you want to see spite, you should take a look at the linen closet." Beck takes me by the elbow, leading me into the primary they used to share. Where the linen closet used to be filled with sheets, blankets, towels, and a whole section of expensive first aid supplies, there's now a refrigerator box beside the shower holding the former contents.

Beck has left him one tiny, thin white towel with his toothbrush on top of it. Not even a tube of toothpaste to be found. And frankly, Sean should find another toothbrush, because I don't know if this one has been used to scrub a toilet or the tile floors or...who knows...something worse.

"You know it's going to take three grown men to carry this box, right?" I ask, attempting to lift it with all my might and failing.

Beck pouts and then holds up four fingers. "You. Jett. Bear. Emmett. We're golden." She steps into the closet. "But hey, don't worry. I'll leave his favorite sweatpants I got for his last birthday." She steps out of the ones she's wearing, and now she's wearing nothing but a crop top and pale pink panties that show off her spectacular ass.

Dear god. I bite back a moan, unable to wrench my eyes away from the incredible sight of her wearing so little as she bends and digs through boxes of clothing on her side of the sprawling closet. I force myself to walk away from the unparalleled view.

"Ready to get back to work on Monday?" I turn away and adjust my hard-on through my basketball shorts.

"Yes and no. I miss my clients, I hear I have a couple of new ones, and I love my job. Being a grief counselor is fulfilling, but I needed the week to feel my own grief. I gave myself exactly seven days to mourn Sean, and, well, it seems like I only needed five or so. Just forget I cried a few minutes ago, okay, because I swear I feel much better now."

"And have you gotten used to the sound of the refrigerator making ice, or do I need to sleep over and slay the ice demons?" Thankfully, my dick settles, and I turn and flash a grin at her.

"It's still pretty quiet," she admits with a shoulder shrug. "I've figured out the ice machine. It's the creaks that get me. Not that I'm not used to sleeping alone, given He Who Shall Not Be Named routinely worked nights."

"I'm game if you ever need."

"Well, maybe I'll take you up on that when I move back into my parents' house. It's been so long since I've lived there, my suite over there is still pink."

I burst into laughter. "What? Pink?"

"Hey, give me a break. I was a teenager back then. At least the suite is nearly as big as this one. The king-size bed will fit nicely. I guess I should start thinking about getting a U-Haul."

"Nah, Bear's got a trailer, and his truck can pull its weight. Remember, we moved Marissa with it a couple of years back?" Beck squishes up her face like she's trying to remember but can't.

"You don't think Bear will mind?" Beck wonders as she bends over to pack up her bedside table into a small box, including several well-worn paperbacks that I can't let the opportunity pass to tease her about.

"Not at all, but I'd hide all that smut." I wink at her, and she smacks my shoulder, hard.

"Never! I love my smut. You can pry it from my cold, dead hands, dude. I've got three more boxes of it sitting in the closet, and some still left to pack from the bookshelf in the living room. Only the discreet covers, of course, since Sean didn't want 'sculpted male chests' on display in *his* living room."

I grunt and shake my head. "Sounds like there were a lot of rules in place for you that I never realized."

It's Beck's turn to shake her head. "Not your fault for not noticing. I didn't talk about it. I thought most of his behavior was normal. Didn't realize how controlling he was, or how deceptive. Love blinded me. I know how to pick 'em, huh?"

I stare at her with the sudden urge to tell her everything.

How close she was to missing out on Sean completely.

How the last ten years were almost *our* shared history.

And how much regret I still carry over the way things went down at that frat party where all three of us first met.

But Beck's been out of a relationship for six days, and no matter how often it wants to tumble out of my mouth, I keep it in. I suffer through it. Because Beck needs to heal, and I don't want her to feel like she doesn't deserve as much time as it takes.

13

ASPYN

The next weekend, after a long week at work, the mid-September weather warms up to nearly eighty degrees, and the urge to barbecue comes over me, so I send a group text, and everyone shows up around 4 p.m. to hang out. It's not the most well-planned; I have to dig the barbecue tools out of a box and then run to the store to buy a bunch of disposable plates, cups, and silverware.

I'm taking Monday and Tuesday off to move, because those are the days Jett is free. Most of my friends have been able to get the time off too, except Emmett, a realtor with out-of-state clients in town those days.

Deacon, Cody, and Jett are in the kitchen, talking about how their favorite NFL team is doing early in the season, while my girlfriends are huddled up in the primary bedroom gossiping. I don't mean to miss out on it, but I'm busy making a pasta salad as a side dish to accompany all the burgers and brats.

When Deacon and the boys quiet down, I overhear Emmett and Bear discussing the best jewelers in the area, so I can only hope the next year or two will be full of weddings.

Emmett's girlfriend Stefanie is finishing up college in Denver, graduating in December, and he's ready to pop the question the night of her graduation.

I hear the ping of the front door and frown. Everyone who's supposed to be here is, but Deacon stands up, pats my shoulder, and disappears off through the dining room to "handle it."

Focused on the food I'm making, I don't even realize all the men have exited the kitchen to the back patio. At first, I think nothing of the bickering voices I hear at the front door. Then, slowly, I creep into the darkened dining room, focusing on the voices. *Uh oh.* Sean is saying something about "my sloppy seconds" as Deacon's features harden, and he stabs a finger into Sean's chest.

"You asshole. I saw her first, you piece-of-shit motherfucker!" Deacon explodes, his face flushed. "I saw her, and she looked like a fucking angel. And then all you did was complain about how she was vanilla and how you hated her hair. *I saw her first!* If you had been a real friend, you would have let me go over to introduce myself, and I would have tried every day to make her happy. But you've only ever loved yourself. You've never given one goddamn about me *or her*! I know you better than anyone else, Sean, and you never really loved Beck. You're a narcissistic, pathetic son-of-a-bitch who's only out for his own gain. And I, for one, loved her pink hair. And everything else about her. Always have. Always will." Deac lowers his voice.

I'm stunned silent, my heart thumping so loudly in my ears I can barely hear Sean's response. I still my breath and eavesdrop.

Sean harumphs. "Sure, you saw her first, but you were too much of a pussy to fight me for her after I called dibs." His voice is loud and angry, and I wince. Dibs? I had been a dibs?

"You'll always be a pussy, Deac. If she ever lets you inside of her, don't forget who was there first! Now, fuck off out of my way. This is my fucking house."

Sean pushes past Deacon as I creep back into the kitchen and pretend I haven't heard a word.

"Where'd the guys go?"

I turn my gaze reluctantly to Sean, standing a few feet away from me in the kitchen with his arms crossed over his chest.

"Jesus, Sean. What are you doing here? I told you I could make this hard on you if you didn't stay away. And I will." I challenge him with a fearless glare.

"Well, I saw all my family and friends here on the Ring doorbell and figured my invitation must've gotten lost in the mail." His voice drips with sarcasm and hatred.

Anger seeps through my veins at the sight of him, and I want to lay him out right there on the tile, but in that moment, I realize the best thing to do is let the guys handle him.

"They're out back." I make my voice as uncaring as possible and give a one-shoulder shrug, averting my eyes as I focus on stirring my pasta salad.

"You could've just said that," Sean snaps, walking past me close enough that his shoulder smacks into mine. The back door shuts after him, and then I spot Deacon silently following him.

I stand at the sink, looking out the window that overlooks the patio and the hot tub. It's wide open to let in the fresh September air, but it also lets in voices. Maybe they don't know it's open, because they stand right underneath it.

Deacon tells Sean in hushed tones, "If Beck lets me inside her, I'll be the one who puts a ring on her finger and comes home to her every night. Only her. She's all the woman I'll ever need. And I'll be the man who gives Beck the children she's always wanted, then be the one who stays forever. You're just a piece of shit who dragged her along because you are a giant fucking child who wanted to have your cake and eat it too. I feel sorry for your baby having you as a father, having to be raised by someone who can never love them, because the only person that you've ever loved is you. Get the fuck out of here man, and don't come back. Consider this *dibs* on the rest of her life, motherfucker."

Sean gets in Deacon's face as my heart thumps in the confines of my ribs. I can't believe the words Deacon just uttered—the confession he'd made to Sean about his love for me. I do the only thing I can think of.

I run. I throw the pasta salad in the fridge, dart into the bedroom, and shut the door like an intruder is pursuing me.

"Jesus, girl. Are you okay?" Tara asks, walking over to me and putting her arm around me. "You look like you've seen a ghost."

"Please tell me there are no ghosts in here," Marissa says as her eyes dart around suspiciously.

"What happened?" Wendy adds.

But I can't tell them. I can't open my mouth and explain to anyone that Sean had called "dibs" on me ten years ago, and that I could have shared the last decade with Deacon, who has apparently been in love with me since he first saw me standing at the punch bowl with my pink locks.

My eyes flutter closed. "Can I—can I get a sec?"

"Sure," Tara tells me, and my girlfriends head single-file out of my bedroom, giving me curious looks. When they're gone, I shut the door, lean my back against it, and slide down it until my knees pull up underneath me. I rest my chin on my knees as tears stream down my cheeks. Had that been the difference between ten unhappy years and ten that could have been wonderful? *Dibs?*

The door rattles when someone knocks on it, and then Deacon's voice loudly calls, "Don't say a word to her! Walk away, Sean, for good. Like you should have done ten goddamn years ago."

The next sound I hear is the slam of the front door, and I bury my head in my hands and try to breathe.

Of course, Deacon loves me.

Now that I've heard it, I realize it's the best-kept, most obvious secret I've ever heard.

I trace the years back in my mind. Our friendship. The thoughtful gifts he'd always given me. The kind words he always had ready for me if I needed it. Subtle hints he'd dropped over the years, suggesting that I could do better than Sean. My own shattered self-worth, the only thing keeping me from listening.

Glancing down at my rose-gold wristwatch, the tears blur. Deacon has always been the most thoughtful man I had ever encountered. I think of all the restaurants I've sat at with Deacon over the years because Sean had been called in to work, or because "something came up." Anniversaries interrupted, late arrivals at Christmas and weddings. Deacon, my dancing partner when Sean was unavailable or just plain refused when I begged.

Deacon, who fished with me, camped with me, took me hiking, included me in basketball games with the guys, fixed my car when it was broken...

Yes—of course, Deacon had loved me all along. I only feel like a fool for not realizing it sooner.

And now I have a choice. I can pretend I didn't hear a word Deacon said at the front hall or on the back patio— pretend like the connection between us is normal. That things are as they've always been; despite knowing the way Deacon has ached for me for ten years.

Or I can put him out of his misery. I mean, he's the best man I've ever met in my life, and if he adores me the way he says he does, it would make me a very lucky woman. But it's so soon after the breakup, isn't it?

It hits me that I'm not as broken-hearted as I should be about Sean, because I've been getting over him for years. Even though I had been in a relationship with him, I learned to manage my expectations. Accepted less than I deserved. Gave a hundred percent and got nothing in return. I had already wrenched my heart away from Sean after having it broken repeatedly, and the proof of him cheating with Nurse Q had been the wake-up call I needed to leave. But I had been leaving him in small ways for years. Nudging out of his arms in bed, turning him down, and shutting myself down emotionally. I'd kept small secrets and internally despised him a bit for the past three years, at least.

That wasn't love, was it?

How many years had it been love? Two? Three? Four? When had it faded into a naïve hope to get back the love we'd lost?

But Deacon. Well, Deacon feels like inevitability.

I look around my boxed-up room and suddenly, I can't wait to be out of this house. It feels like the scene of the crime: where I'd disappeared slowly for eight years, playing a role for Sean with no regard for my needs, dreams, or desires.

Unsure what I'm thinking, I scour through a few boxes and pack my trusty carry-on suitcase, ensuring a couple of smutty books make it in before I zip it up. I set my favorite pillow on top of it.

When I open the door, Deacon's standing outside of it, and he practically falls into the bedroom.

"Hi. Would it be okay if I stayed with you tonight and the next day? Just until I move back in with my parents?" I ask him, pointing to my suitcase. "The truth is, this place feels haunted by the ghost of the girl I used to be, and I need out."

The look on my face must say everything, because Deacon

just nods and gives me a thin smile. He's got a faraway gaze in his eyes that's not typical of him, and we're quiet as we walk into the kitchen.

"You were in there a while. Everyone ate and headed out. Weird vibes, I guess," Deacon tells me as he grabs a plate and methodically begins to reheat my burger and make it just the way I like it, down to three perfect pieces of crunchy iceburg lettuce on top. He piles on a big heaping of my nearly gone, popular pasta salad.

"What would you like to drink?" Deacon asks.

"There's an expensive as shit bourbon open in the cabinet by the fridge," I tell him. Before I know it, he's poured us two glasses, heavy on the rocks.

"Hey, why is your hand bleeding?" I ask, spotting a few drops on his knuckles.

"Oh, well, I broke Sean's nose. He said some nasty things about you that needed a response. He just left. At the time, it felt good to punch the guy, but now I feel numb."

I head to the freezer and grab a soft ice pack I use for migraines, then wrap it in paper towels. "Here, at least ice your knuckles. Did you break anything other than his nose?"

"Our decade-long friendship for good, I imagine. Not that I regret it. You know I picked you, anyway."

Deacon wraps his hand with the ice and winces. I press a kiss to the top of his head as he leans over, my lips in his golden blond hair. Then, I lean my forehead against the back of his neck. Being this close to him comes naturally.

"I understand feeling numb. That's why I need to get out of here. It's not mine. This place was always a conditional home, where I was welcome if I behaved like a good enough girl. I'm done being who someone else wants me to be, but I worry I may have lost myself somewhere along the way." I gulp hard, fear gripping me with a steely fist around my throat.

Massive tears roll down my cheeks as I imagine how it went when Deacon and Sean first spotted me. Sean calling "dibs," Deacon respecting his friend enough to let him pursue me and draw me under his narcissistic spell until I'd given all I had away.

Things Deacon never would have asked me to give.

And then he's off the chair and grabbing me up in his strong arms, pressing my face to his chest.

"I still know exactly who you are, Beck, and I'll remind you until you remember." He whispers the words against my hair, and it warms my aching, frozen heart. Telling me that, despite it all, everything will be okay.

❀ 14 ❀

DEACON

All weekend, Beck is strangely quiet. I'm certain she didn't hear my fight with Sean when he first arrived at the barbecue, or after I'd taken him aside out back on the patio. At first, I'd thought I'd seen movement in the kitchen, but when I ran in to see if Beck overheard me pledging my love for her, the kitchen was empty. If Beck had heard, she hadn't let on.

I'm concerned about her. The little speech she'd given about how she felt she'd lost herself had upset me, because it's one thing to lose a piece-of-shit narcissist and it's another to lose yourself in the process. I know Beck is strong enough to find her way back to her true self, and if she's having a hard time with it, that's what I'm here for.

Sunday afternoon, after a brief rain, I convince her to join me at our favorite lake. Fishing ought to cheer her up, but in the car, "Karma Police" comes on and she puts her head in her hands, no doubt catching her tears. I rest my hand on her thigh with a sad sigh.

"I don't want to live at my parents' house." Beck looks up at me with tears dripping down her cheeks. It takes courage to show someone the depth of your sadness, so when she doesn't wipe away her tears, pride swells for her.

"Then don't. We can find you an apartment if you'd rather. Or..." I trail off. I tell myself I know what I'm doing. "You could stay with me until you decide what's next for you."

"I couldn't possibly intrude on your life, Deac." But something in her voice tells me I should insist.

"Come on. You'd be very much welcome and wanted. Even if you just cook for me a few nights a week, the arrangement will work out well for me. And I get the pleasure of your company." I give her my best, most convincing smile, and she blinks rapidly until she finally nods. But she still looks uncertain.

"If you're sure, I would prefer that over my parents' house. It's just so big and empty. Cavernous, really. I know it's supposed to be for me, but I can't see myself living there before I have kids to fill the bedrooms."

I nod with sympathy. "I get it. My house is much too big to be alone in, too, and you'll have your choice of rooms. You bringing the bed with you?"

"Hell yes. It's expensive, with an adjustable base. Heavy as shit, but if there's room on the trailer, then yes." Beck opens the window, letting the breeze dry her tears, and turns her face up to the sunshine.

"Then we should put you in the upstairs primary. I haven't gotten around to getting a bedroom set, but your things should fit nicely in there." I pull up to the marina and park the truck. Thinking about being under the same roof as Beck makes my spine stiffen and my hands tremble slightly. *How the hell am I going to exercise restraint with her in such close proximity?* Just our nearness in this truck is driving me crazy.

I come around to her side of the truck and open the door, offering her my hand to help her down. It's not that she needs it; she's five-eight and doesn't struggle with the height of my truck, but I'm overwhelmed by the need to touch her, even in a small way. She takes my hand, and she doesn't drop it right away.

Beck has a thoughtful look on her face. She avoids eye contact with me and shuffles her feet against the loose gravel. "Deac—" she starts but hesitates. Her tongue peeks out to wet her bottom lip as she tilts her head slightly from side to side, as if she's weighing her options, perhaps rehearsing her next words.

"Just say yes, Beck. Say yes." I interrupt with one last attempt to convince her.

"Yes, I'm going to say yes." Beck lets out a long sigh of what sounds like relief, and as we load our arms up with our fishing poles, tackle box, and cooler, she bumps into me accidentally and then presses the sweetest kiss to my cheek. I almost turn my head, but she pulls away and adds, "Thank you doesn't cut it. I'll always owe you for this."

You don't owe me anything.

"You can repay me by helping clean out my mother's closet," I smile, though my stomach turns. I've stood in it several times now, feeling sad and overwhelmed, and I wish Beck would come and take everything she wants so I can put the rest on consignment. Or maybe I'll invite Marissa, Wendy, and Tara over to scrounge through it before I do that.

"Of course I will," Beck says breezily with a big smile. "Especially if she has more incredible jewelry like this piece." She holds up her free hand and admires the first ring I'd placed on her finger. If I have it my way, it won't be the last. I shudder at the strength of my feelings for this woman; my mind filled with curiosity about what kind of diamond ring she would want. If she even wants a diamond. Maybe she's a ruby kind of girl or sapphire.

"Did you hear what I said?" Beck asks.

"Nope. Repeat?" I follow her to our usual dock, passing up

some expensive boats that I envy. A boat is the goal I've been saving for a long time, but diamond rings don't come cheap either, so I may have to make a choice.

Okay, I'm being ridiculous. I should probably date Beck before I worry about a ring and a proposal.

"Bro!" Beck yells. "Pay attention! I'm here chatting away while you are on a different planet. Has your consciousness been abducted by aliens?"

I laugh while Beck sets her things down and sighs. "It's hot today. Shit."

"Hot. Yes." Why am I speaking in monosyllabic words?

I pull my shirt over my head and deposit it on the back of the camp chair Beck has set up for me. I don't miss the sharp inhale when Beck turns her eyes to my chest. If nothing else, she admires my body, and the feeling is decidedly mutual.

"Are you trying to distract me from the fish? You want to get the bigger catch today, huh?" Beck flirts. She flirts! Dear baby Jesus.

A slow smile spreads to my face. "How many times do I have to tell you it's not a competition, you little flirt?"

"If I have to keep looking at those divots between your six-pack abs, I'm in trouble." Beck winks at me, and I want to hoist her up out of her camp chair and put her hand on my abs to discover what she's been staring at.

"So, you want me to put the shirt back on?" I act confused as she laughs and balls up my shirt before throwing it at me. She misses, and it falls off the other side of the dock into the water. I reach down to rescue it and pull it out, dripping wet.

I cluck my tongue at her. "Guess the bare chest stays."

"I'll pretend that bothers me." Beck grins as I settle in the chair beside her and bait my hook. She's already got her pole in the water, and she pops the cooler and pulls out two cold beers, setting one in my mesh cupholder.

"Thanks, doll face." I cast my fishing pole, rest it between my knees, twist open the beer, and get comfortable. "It's good to hear you laugh. You seem lighter than you did this morning."

"Woke up on the wrong side of the bed, and the rain didn't help. It's always good to get out in the sun and near a body of water. I'm so tempted to jump in."

"The water's chilly," I warn her, having just wrangled my shirt out of it.

"I know. But it's hot today, and I'm not a wuss."

"Well, do what you want. I'll watch."

"I bet you'll watch," Beck snorts. "You're such a dude."

"Guilty." I shrug. "Can't believe your move-in day is tomorrow. What are we going to do with all the extra furniture you have? Come to think of it, I have plenty of space in the garage, and there's room in the basement for a living room set. I just haven't put any time into that yet. We could make it a cozy family room down there."

"Sounds good. I'd love that. Jesus, I hope we don't run into Sean tomorrow or the next day as I move out. I unplugged the Ring camera because, well, fuck him."

I snort and take a long pull from my beer. "Fuck him for sure."

We fish, and I rake in more than she does, but she's a good sport about it. When I think we're about to leave, Beck runs a few docks down where we haven't seen any sign of people, and she sheds her shorts and top and jumps into the water with a screech.

I'm pretty sure it's that moment when she realizes the distance between the dock and the water, and the fact that there are no ladders to help her pry herself out of the cold waves. She grimaces for a second, and then she's all smiles.

"Water's nice!" Beck calls.

She floats on her back wearing a lacy navy-blue bra and

matching panties, but at least these have material over the ass, so she's in the equivalent of a bikini.

"I'd jump in, but then neither of us will be able to get out."

"Come on, you're strong. You'll be fine." Beck splashes the water next to her. And because I'm insane and in love with the girl, I shed my cargo shorts and cannonball in. The water feels like being pricked with tiny needles all over, and my face flushes with surprise.

"You didn't tell me it was so c-c-cold," I chatter as I reach for Beck. "Y-you're crazy!"

She does a back flip in the water and comes up sputtering with her hair all over the place, and I get a glimpse of the nineteen-year-old Beck I'd met the night of the frat party. In the water, she's youthful and free, and I like the way it looks on her.

I pull her up to my chest and wrap my arms around her. "You remind me of how you looked when we met the first night. Minus the pink hair."

Beck presses her face to my shoulder, and her lips are freezing as she rests against me. "You're the only one who loved the pink hair on me. Other than me."

"Who cares what anyone thinks? If you liked it, you should do it again." I cup the back of her head and then lean to press a kiss to her forehead. "You know I'll back all your plays."

"That's sweet, but I'm fr-freezing, so how about you start with getting up to the dock and pulling me out of here?" Beck's teeth chatter as she speaks.

It's an impressive feat, but I manage to get up on the dock thanks to brute strength alone. I carefully extract Beck from the water, and when I pull her, she ends up on top of me, sprawled across the dock. She giggles, and I can't help but join in, and we become a mass of appendages and laughter under the last day of September sky.

When we return to our things, Beck turns her back to me and unclasps her bra, facing the setting sun. She sits on the dock facing away from the couple of stragglers we'd passed on our way in; they're far enough behind us that they won't see her.

"You can sit with me," she calls casually.

"No, I can't." It sounds like a confession.

"Ah, yes, Deac. I remember you once telling me to 'put my tits away.'" Beck giggles.

"I was trying to be a good guy."

"You are the best guy," Beck tells me softly. "Will you hand me my hairbrush? It's in my purse."

I reach into her small purse and find what she's looking for. Instead of tossing it and it possibly ending up in the lake, I hand it to her and finally sit down beside her.

"It's tough not to look," I admit as she works her brush through her hair, starting at her tangled ends. "You're gorgeous, Beck." It feels like a dangerous admission.

"I think what you're saying is my boobs are gorgeous." She giggles. "And I never wear a bra around the house. You'll be bored with them after I've been living with you a while, I promise."

With her face turned away from me, I trace a fingertip up the top of her thigh, electricity jolting between us as I creep ever higher. "No, Beck, believe me, that day will never come." I let my hand rest on her thigh, not too high up, but not on her knee either.

Goosebumps give her away.

I close my eyes and try to breathe. Her soft skin under my fingertips distracts the hell out of me, and I really should pull my hand away, but...god, just touching her is heavenly.

When I open my eyes, Beck is staring at me. There's

curiosity in her gaze, like I'm a puzzle she's trying to put together but can't quite remember how it's supposed to look.

I reach for her chin and tip it upward, and I whisper, "You're beautiful, Beck. All of you." Hand still on her chin, I glance down and take in those full, perky breasts, the light pink of her pebbled nipples, and I can't hold in a groan.

"Next time I tell you to put those away, ignore me," I practically whimper, dropping her chin, and then I stare straight ahead at the sun gently dipping behind the mountains.

"What a beauty," I whisper, my meaning two-fold.

"The sky is perfect. A golden swirl." I can hear the smile in Beck's voice as she leans her head against me.

Then, suddenly, from behind us, "Excuse me, young lady. May I please ask you to cover up so I can access my boat?"

15

ASPYN

I'm horrified when a sweet older man asks me to cover up. Right away, Deac hands me my shirt, and I toss it over my head with apologies on my lips.

"Oh, no need to apologize. I remember the impulsivity of youth with fondness," the man tells me as I jump up to my feet and whirl around to come face to face with him.

He's the cutest older man: a head full of silver hair, hard-won wrinkles especially around his eyes, and he's slight, maybe five-foot-five. His smile is warm, and it reaches his brown eyes.

"How old are you kids?" he asks.

"Twenty-nine. Not so young," I laugh. "I'm Aspyn, and this is Deacon. I'm sorry again."

"I'm Hans." He speaks with the slightest of German accents. "I've seen you here before, fishing together. You seem like nice kids. I remember the days of nude sunbathing myself. This lake was cleaner thirty-five years ago, though. That was back when I met my late wife, Mary. Here, in fact. She was the guest on another man's boat."

Hans gives us a crooked smile that I find charming, and I send him an encouraging one back.

"So, how did you win her over?" I ask.

"We became friends. I waited for him to make a mistake and swooped in. I'm not proud of it, but I won her heart. Before that, I believe I was in what you kids call 'the friend zone.' I wasn't a man of means back then, but she saw through those trappings into my soul."

Tears swim in my eyes. "That's beautiful, Hans. You said... your late wife? I'm so terribly sorry."

Hans frowns and nods. "Thank you. She fought the cancer with everything she had. Three different times, she won. The fourth was too much for her frail body. We spent our last night on this little yacht six months ago, a few weeks before hospice came in to help give her peace."

I'm going to sob for this old man, aren't I? I put my hand over my mouth and try not to embarrass myself.

Instead, what comes out is, "Deacon just lost his mom to cancer a few months ago. It's a beast. Again, I don't have the words to express how sorry I am."

"I'm sorry too, Deacon," Hans tells him as Deacon visibly gulps. "The truth is, I've come to say goodbye to this ol' boat. Without her, 'Love in the Sun' is just loneliness. I'm getting ready to sell her in the spring."

I glance at the name of the boat in dark purple letters, and it tugs at my heartstrings.

"I'd like to take her out one last time before winter comes. Would you kids like to jump on board? We'll be losing sunlight here soon, but the view of the stars from the center of the lake is priceless."

Even though we need to get up early for moving day, Deacon and I can't resist Hans' charm, so we hop on to Love in the Sun, and Hans gives us the grand tour. It's not a big yacht, but it has a living area, kitchenette, and a room with a queen-sized bed below deck, along with a fully-functioning bathroom I beg to use. Up top, well-taken-care-of, shiny purple leather circular bench seats surround a round table where Hans tells us he and Mary played a great deal of card games over the years. We settle down into the leather seats while Hans drives the boat out to the middle of the lake.

The sunset is spectacular ahead of us, with the colors of dusk lighting up the skies in orange as bright as flames, fuchsia pinks, and even a bit of violet swirls. Despite how pretty it is, I keep catching Deacon staring at me, though he looks away every time I catch his eyes.

Hans turns off the boat, and we float, the clear blue lake stretching out on all sides of us; nothing but water and sky and mountains in all directions.

"Purple is Aspyn's favorite color," Deacon tells Hans as he motions to the leather we're sitting on and the purple LED track lights shining bright.

"It was Mary's as well. I had this boat designed with her in mind. She loved it. Going out on the lake was our favorite thing to do together, and I'm afraid now that she's gone, I'll not be able to stomach coming out here alone." Hans pulls out his flip phone and takes a couple of photos of the sun setting in the distance. "I feel very small when I'm out here. Maybe too small," Hans admits.

"Me too." I nod.

Deacon is quiet but wears a thoughtful expression. "Sir, if I give you my number, will you call me come spring and let me know what your asking price is on this beautiful boat? I've been considering buying one for a long time, and by spring, I'll probably have a good nest egg."

Hans dismisses him with a wave of the hand. "You two remind me of me and my wife, and I think this good old boat would be happy in your hands. You'll take it, with a discount, in April, if you're still able."

Deacon looks overwhelmed by Hans' generosity, and they shake hands while Deacon expresses his gratitude.

We stay out on the lake until the stars twinkle above us, not a cloud in the sky, reminding us how we're both nothing and everything. Deacon reaches over and entwines his fingers with mine as I lie flat on the bench seat and stare up. A shooting star zaps across the night sky, and Deacon whispers, "Make a wish."

But I have everything I need, so I steal a suitable answer from beauty pageant queens and passionately wish for world peace, or at least peace within myself. That's where peace really starts, anyway. And it feels like I'm close to it, as the dark blues and grays of the night sky paint a perfect canvas from which the stars shine endlessly, burning a million times more powerfully than fire, some alive, some dead, all stunning no matter the phase. I sigh in wonder.

We stay up too late on the boat, eating snacks Hans brought and drinking the Chardonnay his wife had left downstairs on their last trip together.

When Deacon and I walk back to the truck, his free hand slides into mine, and he doesn't drop it until he opens the passenger door for me and gently closes it behind me.

My heart feels cracked open in the best way—like it's almost ready to let love in, though fear persists.

That night, I can't sleep, so I knock lightly on Deacon's door and ask, "Are you still up?" in a low tone.

"Sorta," comes his muffled answer. "You okay?" His head pops up from beneath a pillow, his hair standing on end. I fight the urge to laugh.

"I'm okay, just can't fall asleep. And your house is full of new noises," I confess, stepping into his room. Into the quiet darkness, I add, "Can I sleep next to you?"

I worry he'll say no, but he simply holds up the covers and whispers, "Climb in, babe."

So, I curl up on my side near Deacon, who lies shirtless in basketball shorts beside me.

"Closer," I whisper.

He inches nearer.

"Closer," I whisper again.

"Just come here, woman." Deacon throws his arm out to the side and then wraps it around me, yanking me near as I lay my cheek on his warm, well-muscled chest. When my hand rests on his abdomen, my fingers tremble a bit, nervous being so close to the man I've called my bestie for so many years.

"I can hear your anxiety from here," Deacon tells me. "Just feel up my abs. It's fine. I know you wanna."

He makes me laugh, and my fingers drift around his hard stomach, discovering those lovely dips between muscles I'd only seen with my eyes until now. Deacon lightly groans as I slide my hand back up to his pec and back down to his stomach. I trace his hip bone, noting the V-shape of his musculature, every touch awakening something in me that had been sleeping for some time.

I breathe heavier, unsure if this was the best idea. In the guest room, I hadn't been able to shut my brain off, and I was still so dazzled from our night out on the boat with Hans that I couldn't calm myself down. Being in such close proximity to Deacon only speeds my heart rate and sends my stomach lurching.

"Shh," Deac whispers against my ear. "Relax. It's just you and me, Beck."

And I eventually do relax and fade into a dreamless sleep, waking up before the alarm the next morning, all tangled up in Deacon. He's spooning me from behind with an arm beneath my neck that I'm using for a pillow, his other arm draped around my waist. His top leg has captured both of my legs beneath it. And truth be told? It's the most secure I've felt in ages, his body against mine, his breath steady in my ear. I try not to move a muscle, though my ear feels like it has fallen asleep from resting on his bicep.

I move just enough that Deacon stirs and groans, "Mmm," from behind me. My nightshirt has crept up beneath my breasts, leaving my belly and panties exposed. His hand moves to my stomach and rests there warmly, as he sighs and shifts to get closer in his sleep.

Only now, I can feel his morning erection pressing against my ass, and I know one thing I didn't before: he's incredibly well-endowed. I fight to ignore those thoughts as I wiggle to free myself, fruitlessly, feeling Deacon move even closer in his sleep.

"Well, this is awkward," I whisper beneath my breath. *Or is it exactly where you belong, Aspyn?* I raise a good point, so I let sleep capture me again despite my ear throbbing with pins and needles. When I awake again, we're mostly in the same position, except Deacon's hand has risen and he's cupping one of my breasts.

A groan tears from my lips as he moves restlessly against me, still hard, still pressed against my ass. It's a sensory experience unlike any other. My heart beats a crescendo in my chest as Deacon snores in my ear. The hitch in my breath tells me I don't exactly mind the situation, and when his fingers move just slightly, they graze my nipple, which pebbles under his touch. I ache, and I must arch my back because my ass pushes closer to his hardness.

You didn't sleep with Sean the last three months of your relationship.

My sex drive reminds me that I'm horribly unfulfilled as I moan softly and circle my hips back against Deacon, something wild inside me taking over as my sleepy body reacts to his. I take slow breaths in my nose and out my mouth to try to calm the longing, but I feel somehow empty, and I'm dying to be filled with Deacon.

No. Don't ruin your friendship. Don't complicate things. Things are too wonderful as they are to change anything now.

Deacon's hand moves down my belly and rests at the top of my panties, and he murmurs something low in his throat. He's got to be awake by now. The question is, do I care?

I gasp at the way my clit throbs at his nearness.

"Morning," he whispers, inching even closer to me.

His hand is still dangerously low on my belly. I burn with desire, but quickly decide to run.

"I should go get dressed." He drops his hand and lets me stand up.

"Sorry about my hand placement," he whispers. "Is it time to get up?"

"The alarm will go off in five minutes. It's moving day!" I feign enthusiasm, run off to the guest room, and then I touch myself until I come hard, my back arching and head falling into my mound of pillows.

With a rosy face, I brush my teeth, my slightly-wavy hair, and then pull on a grungy outfit and meet Deacon downstairs in the kitchen. Since we already moved my espresso machine in, he has an iced espresso ready for me, topped with whipped cream, just the way I like it.

When our eyes meet, there's something that passes between us that's new. It nearly sizzles.

I gulp and say, "Thank you," as I take the glass mug and guzzle. There's still a pulse and throb between my thighs, and my breath comes out heavy as we fall into silence, drinking our respective beverages at the kitchen table. Deacon opens a package of donuts and hands me a plate. They're my favorite kind, the ones with powdered sugar and crumbles on top.

Deacon stands, grabs a glass of milk for me, and smiles as he hands it over.

"They really are better dunked," I insist.

He leans and kisses the top of my head and then sits down at my side. "Big day ahead. You ready for this?"

My heart beats out of my chest as he stares at me. What has come over me?

"I'm beyond ready. After I have another donut, let's go do this." I grin at him, and he reaches his hand toward my face and cups my cheek, staring at me adoringly.

"You've got this, Beck. Today's the day to leave the past behind. By the end of the day, your bedroom set will be in the extra primary bedroom, and your monstrosity of a blender will be taking up half of the extra space on my countertop."

"I packed the margarita fixings, and I labeled the box well. We can celebrate with margs tonight!"

I flash him a gleeful look and dunk my donut for exactly eleven seconds before shoving it in my mouth.

"Did I ever tell you that you eat like a T. rex?" Deacon side-eyes me as my cheeks puff out with the large bite I've just taken.

"Heyyy," I say around the donut, but it proves his point. "Don't make me laugh!" I practically choke, taking a few more sips of milk until the donut is more manageable, and I finally swallow.

"Sorry about the mean, accurate thing I said," Deac tells me, patting my shoulder as he stands up and texts something on his phone. That's when it occurs to me. If I wait too long to act on the feelings I have for this man, I could lose him entirely. How the hell would I feel if he moved on without me?

Fear paralyzes me, and I stare straight ahead, my back straight and stiff. But he's been waiting on me for a decade...

can't I count on him to wait a little longer? Wait until I'm ready?

"You okay?" Deacon senses my subtle mood change.

"Yeah, it's nothing."

But it's not nothing. Heat surges through my body when I stand up and look at Deacon in his tight black T-shirt, remembering how his muscles had felt beneath my hand last night. Remembering how his body had fit perfectly with mine when we woke up pasted together under the covers.

I shake my head to clear it, adding, "Never mind."

Deacon tilts his head, and I feel certain I'm see-through and he's plucking the thoughts from my brain because he looks almost satisfied as he says, "Suit yourself. Should we get going?"

We part ways to go in different cars, and when we arrive at the house I used to share with Sean, he's thankfully not in there anywhere. Our friends arrive, and then Jett carefully backs the trailer up the long driveway and opens it up. Everyone jumps in to help, and before we know it, the trailer is full of furniture and boxes. At the last minute, I pack Sean's PlayStation, which had been a Christmas gift from me, and add it to the old Wii I still love to exercise on in a big box, then toss it in my car. The trailer is full by noon.

An hour later, I've cleared out everything I cared to carry with me into the next chapter of my life.

This is the end of ten years of settling. I'll never put myself last again.

I peer at myself in the full-length mirror on the front hall closet, and I see my own reflection. I look lighter, brighter, and happier than I have in ages, and I say to myself, "My happy era is next."

With that in mind, I set my key on the kitchen counter, put my hand in Deacon's, then slam the door behind me so hard the "Welcome" wreath I made in a crafting class clatters off the door. Deacon grabs it at the last minute, and he insists we take it with us.

I don't so much as look over my shoulder at the home I'm leaving behind.

We drive separately back to Deacon's house, about eight miles from Sean's, and I wonder if I'll ever take this particular drive again. None of my friends live near Sean.

A new barista somewhere was going to have to get to know my favorite order wherever I ended up long-term, and I'd have to find a new neighborhood pub for Thirsty Thursday with the girls.

The thought excites me. I'm ready to usher in the new to replace the stagnant old haunts that do nothing but remind me of ten years lost.

By the time Deacon and I arrive, our friends have unloaded most of the boxes onto the lawn, and they're waiting for us to direct the furniture into their new spots. We join in and ease the living room furniture down the steps into the basement, while my bed and all my things go up to the spacious secondary suite on the second floor.

By four, the girls are helping me make my bed.

"Seems like this will be a cozy living arrangement," Tara tells me as she smooths out my duvet and fluffs a pillow. "All your stuff fits perfectly."

"Yeah, I'm glad Deac is allowing me to be here." I smile.

"Allowing you? He's probably thrilled. Don't you know he claims to hate living alone?" Marissa asks.

I shake my head, unaware. "Well, anyway, this will be a nice crash pad before I figure out what's next for me." I shrug. "I can't see it being forever."

Yes, you can. If you're honest with yourself about your feelings... You can.

We climb onto the bed and gossip for a while, until Deacon shouts, "Pizza!" and we scramble to get downstairs and fill up our hungry bellies. It occurs to me as I look around the living room—I have the best friends. They'd all taken off work and eagerly shown up to lift heavy boxes and furniture and get me settled into my new temporary arrangement. And they'd done so happily.

I pass out cold beers to everyone and then propose a toast. "To the best friends a girl could ever ask for, and...new beginnings."

We clink beers, and now it's time to party.

16

DEACON

Beck is a little quiet for the next several days, and I catch myself often wondering what she's thinking. It feels like just yesterday she told me everything without holding back, and now I get the feeling that something has changed. That she's more deliberate with her words. And I just hope I've not done something to make her clam up or make her uncomfortable. I think back to almost a week ago in bed, that morning when things got a little out of hand, and I assume that has a bit to do with it.

It's wonderful living under the same roof as Beck. The aroma of rosemary and thyme fills the air on Friday night when I arrive home from work. I walk into the kitchen, glance at the golden-brown chicken pot pie sitting on the stovetop, its crust cooling. Beck stands in a flour-dusted apron that proclaims "NOT YOUR MAMA" alongside a fiery pepper, leaning over the sink, clattering dishes as she washes them. Her golden hair, a wild halo, is messily streaked with flour.

I sneak up on her without meaning to, and I slip my arms

around her waist. She startles, dropping the soapy dish from her hands, and then calms and leans back against me. I kiss the side of her head.

"Hey, doll face. Chicken or turkey pot pie?"

"Chicken. With plenty of peas, which I know are your favorite green vegetable." Beck sighs and wrenches herself from my grasp. "Just give me a minute to get more presentable."

Beck yanks off the apron. I reach for her hand to stop her from leaving. "Aspyn Beckett, why do I feel like you're running away from me?"

She stops in her tracks and sends me a wide-eyed glance with her big, doe eyes. I watch her gulp and search for words, but eventually, she denies it. "I'm not. I'm just a mess today. Hard day at work. Got twin six-year-olds who lost both their parents and are now living with their aunt. You know I'm not fond of kids."

So, she's had a bad day. But I also know she's not telling me everything. I let her shrug free and run up the stairs. Then, I hear the water run and the unmistakable sound of Beck humming an old Bryan Adams tune that always cheers her up.

Jagged lightning, almost blinding, suddenly illuminates the kitchen, making me jump as I hear Beck curse upstairs. I glance out the window, the cold glass against my cheek, as I spot the black clouds above. The air is heavy with the near-constant crackling in bright zigzags. A cold wind whips past the windowpanes, rattling them. I don't mind a good Rocky Mountain storm, but the chill in the air today is already biting at only fifty degrees.

October had just arrived with its crisp, cool temperatures. The scent of burning autumn leaves hangs in the air despite the rain. I've noticed Beck each night silently padding down the steps and stealing my soft, worn hoodies from the hall closet. She'd staunchly rejected Sean's clothes; mine were fair game. Hey, as long as it keeps her warm. She always returns them in the morning, but her strawberry citrus scent lingers, an intoxicating smell. I just wish that she'd use my arms and body heat instead.

We have a nice dinner, totally delicious right down to a homemade pie crust. I'd eaten half the entire pie before throwing in the proverbial fork and then jumped up to finish cleaning the kitchen.

I call, "Thanks for dinner," but Beck has already disappeared to her room. She's up there for about an hour while I clean up and get comfortable on the couch.

Finally, she descends the stairs, her voice a soft question amongst the thunder. "Movie?"

I find the one she wants to watch. The flickering light of the new sexy Western casts shadows as we settle in—her in the worn recliner, me sprawled on the couch. My focus blurs, lost in the yearning to brush a stray strand of hair from Beck's face, to feel the warmth of her nestled against me. I don't know why she's so far away from me, why we aren't huddled together on this stormy night, but the question preoccupies me. I thought she was interested in me, but with the way she's pulled back, I'm entirely uncertain.

The movie's plot is a backdrop to my overwhelming urge to touch her. I want to pick her up and plop her in the middle of my bed, strip her bare, and place my hot lips all over her skin.

With a yawn, Beck announces she's heading to bed as soon as the credits roll—I can't believe we've gotten through the entire movie. I couldn't tell you the most basic plot points, since I was somewhere else while Beck watched.

She walks past me to the bottom of the stairs, thinks better of it, then turns and presses a kiss to my forehead that I wish were so much more. But I'll take this. I'll take a whisper of her lips against my skin and her whispered "Goodnight."

After her door closes, it's only a minute before her light goes off, and I sit there pining after her until I finally turn in. Sleep eludes me.

17

ASPYN

I take a half-day off to get tested for STIs at my gynecologist's office the next day. Given Sean's constant cheating, I had left myself open to infections and diseases, naively thinking my ex-boyfriend was loyal.

I feel like the luckiest woman in the world when I get an all-clear, though they've sent out an HIV test and it won't be in for a few days. I'm not worried about that as much, since Sean gets tested every six months, working in the emergency room, sometimes more, and he always comes back clean. After the doctor clears me, I practically skip to my Durango, then to the coffee shop to meet up with Tara, who had asked me to hang out.

"How's married life?" I ask as we sit down, me with a matcha latte and Tara with a mocha. Her eyes practically sparkle as she tells me how in love she is with Cody. After an appropriate amount of time, Tara turns the question around on me and asks how life is going without her "skeevy" brother.

I sip my matcha and shrug. "Honestly, I've never felt freer than I did the moment I tossed his house key down on the dining room table and slammed that front door. I know he's your brother, so please don't take offense, but now I know what I'm worth. Sean never deserved a minute of my time. Now, I'm filled with this renewed sense of hope, like the possibilities are endless. The last five years were so angsty and stagnant with Sean, I'm ready to live without the emotional manipulation and mind-twisting."

Tara gives me an empathetic smile and a nod. "I get that. Part of me never understood why you would put up with such bad behavior from my brother. I'm so glad you've resolved to find bigger and better, but I also can't stop thinking of the man that's right in front of you and has been this entire time."

I drop my gaze to the table, my ears getting hot as she continues.

"When you told me what Deacon said to Sean about calling dibs on the rest of your life...honestly, it was the most romantic thing I've ever heard, much more romantic than Cody's proposal, even. So, how is all that going?"

I feel tears rush to my eyes, but I try to blink them back. "Honestly? I've never felt so wanted or so overwhelmed by someone's feelings for me. There's no one I trust more. I mean, he's Deacon. I think back on our history and see all the times he's been there for me without hesitation. Remember that time Sean got wasted on our anniversary? My phone was dead, so Deacon drove to the restaurant and had dinner with me. And then he took me to a drive-in movie to see an anniversary screening of *Titanic*? He didn't even laugh when Jack faded away into the water. I'm almost sure I saw his eyes get teary."

I let out a long exhale. "He knew it was my favorite film. He knows all the details, because he's been listening all along."

"Because he's been in love with you since you were nineteen. And his biggest regret is not throwing down the gauntlet with Sean to win your heart. He made that clear at the barbecue. So, now that you're living there, has anything happened between you two?"

I briefly tell Tara about our boat adventure with Hans and the fact that Deacon intends to buy it in the spring. But mostly I relay how easy it had been not to correct Hans when he assumed we were a couple.

"But nothing sexy?" Tara blinks rapidly and twirls her hand in the air as if to say, "get to the good stuff."

I sip my drink, groan, and admit, "No. Had to get tested for STIs this morning since your brother has never met a nurse he didn't want to dip his dick into."

Tara snorts. "I can't even stand up for him. He's just that bad."

"Well, if you remember, Deacon doesn't exactly know that *I* know what he said to Sean. I ran off before he could discover me overhearing the conversation. So, I haven't exactly told him I heard." I grimace and close my eyes to avoid Tara's judgment.

She slaps the table in front of me, none-too-gently, and demands to know, "Why, Aspyn? Why? You're willing to let him suffer through thinking he's in love alone for even longer than the ten years he already has? How many days are you going to let this stretch out between you two?"

Tears blur my vision, and I swipe angrily at them for being so quick to show up.

"Jesus Christ, girl. I know it's soon after Sean, but this is Deacon, not some new guy you just met. What the hell are you waiting for?" Tara delivers the final punch, and... knock out.

All I do is shrug one shoulder and avert my eyes. "Until the moment is right? Until the ache of Sean's infidelity begins to wane?" I finger the bottom of my fishtail braid and frown.

"How's that going for ya?"

I bite my lip, not expecting Tara to be so forceful or blunt. She's usually so gentle.

"Well, I waver between trying to see in retrospect all the red flags and clues Sean must have left me, while conversely picturing Deacon in all sorts of sexy scenarios I'm way too shy to initiate."

Tara chortles as she fiddles with her three-carat engagement ring, spinning it on her finger with a nod of understanding. "Listen, Sean's a good liar. I wouldn't have known either, and he's my brother. I should have been able to see through his bullshit, too. It's like I don't know him at all. He's two years older, so as a kid, I grew up admiring him, and now it's like this giant let-down to see him for who he is."

"I know it's not easy seeing Sean in the correct light, but I'm so grateful you drew a line in the sand with him and refused to turn against me. You've been a constant in my life for so long, I'm not sure how I'd manage without you, Tar. Eight years is a pretty good stretch of friendship, and I won't, can't lose you." I cover her hand with mine on the table and squeeze.

"You don't have to. I'll figure out a way to be an aunt to Sean's crotch goblin and stay your friend. The whole family is up in arms, totally disgusted with Sean, but you know how it goes. Mom and Dad will change their minds once the baby comes, and they get to be grandparents for the first time."

I sniffle and wipe my face with the backs of my hands as emotion hits me right in the stomach. "I'm going to miss them, the same way I miss Lillian. Deacon and I still need to sort her closet, but I sense it's too soon for him."

Tara shakes her head adamantly. "Stop talking like that. As soon as you can handle being in the same room with Sean without punching him or verbally eviscerating him, you're coming back to our Christmas party. After all, I make the guest list." Tara beams brightly and does a shoulder shimmy that makes me giggle.

"When Deacon punched Sean—"

"And broke his nose so bad he needs to have surgery," Tara interrupts.

I cackle in delight. "What? Surgery?!"

"He had a broken nose as a kid and should have gotten surgery to fix his deviated septum eons ago. This punch pushed him over the edge, and now he can't wait any longer to fix it. He's got surgery scheduled for next week." Tara hides her grin with her hand. "Oh, I'm for sure going to hell, because when I found out, I almost peed my pants laughing."

"See you there! Anyway, I'd love to come back to the party. I'm sure his mistress will be present and ready to pop by then, though." The thought of it turns my stomach.

"Hey. I believe in your ability to ignore them and focus on your happiness. By then, you and Deac will be together, and that will take precedence over everything else. All the bad memories will fade, and you'll be able to see Sean again and only mildly want to throttle him. Or maybe you'll want to thank him for finally fucking up bad enough to push you into Deacon's arms. Where you always should have been. Sean and Deacon will figure things out, or they won't. Deac is a part of our family, and so are you. You'll both be at the Christmas party. Oh, hey! Cody got you this!"

Tara digs into her oversized purse and pulls out a small box containing a familiar, beautifully frosted cupcake with a cherry on top.

"Bananas Foster?" I ask, in awe. When she gives a nod of confirmation, I do a happy dance in my chair.

"That hubby of yours is too sweet. Please thank him for me," I tell Tara as I accept the cupcake. Cody travels for work and nestled by the train station is my favorite cupcake shop, where this one was purchased. It's my all-time favorite dessert.

"Please tell me I can eat this right now!" I grab the package and wait for Tara's okay to rip it open. I want to sniff it like a total lunatic and then shove it in my mouth without a fork and knife.

Tara tells me, "Do it to it, girl," and I pull off a chunk and shove it in my mouth so hard, the frosting almost goes up my nostrils. Tara's kind enough to jump up and grab napkins for me as I close my eyes in total pleasure, my eyelashes fluttering as I savor the flavors on my tongue.

Sean had a way of making me feel guilty for enjoying dessert as a woman who dared to be a size bigger than he thought I should be. He regularly threw away my leftovers from restaurants I loved, his way of telling me to avoid the carbs. I could never be skinny enough or big-boobed enough for him, despite having normal-sized, full breasts in proportion to the rest of my frame. The fucker spent eight years pressuring me to get a boob job.

I pull out my phone and text Cody to thank him.

"I just told your hubby I love him. Don't mind me. That was the most incredible cupcake." A sigh escapes me. "Tara, I feel good. I really, really do."

"Well, great. That's what you deserve. You were a great girlfriend to my brother, and he should have treated you like the goddamn queen you are—" she glances over to see a young girl and her mom glare her way for the foul language and lowers her voice. "The lovely queen you are. And I think you know who's going to treat you better. Who's going to give you the world. Even a boat, it seems."

Tara reaches across the table and takes my hands. "Girl, just let things work out, will you? How can I convince you to look at Deacon and see him for the love of your life he's going to be?"

I press my lips together into a thin line, my heart beating faster as I remember the morning I awoke pressed against him, and all the flutters and feelings that had overtaken me that day. He was like a cupcake I couldn't wait to dig into, but I'd been trying not to eat it for so long, I don't know where to begin. Okay, that's a terrible analogy. But he is.

"Don't tell him I know," I beg Tara, my hands held together as if I'm praying. "Please, please don't. Let me take a little more time to get my head screwed on right."

Tara grumbles and calls me a pussy under her breath, and the mom and tot nearby move to another table.

"Congrats, you drove them away with your filthy language," I tease her.

"Good, because I don't need that kind of negativity. You need to nut up and just kiss the man, will you? Tell him you heard what he had to say and that you're intrigued. He's waited so long for you. God forbid you wait too long only to find he's moved on." She bites her lip as she shrugs. "Hey, it could happen. He's dated a bit in the last decade. Pining has to have an expiration date—don't wait until it's the day after."

My heart twists painfully, and I press my forehead against the table, wanting to bang my head on it but not wanting to cause a scene.

"What if I suck at being his girlfriend? What if I disappoint him?" I worry aloud, my temples aching.

"Think about how well you treated my shitbag brother and ask yourself how much more you'd spoil the actual love of your life."

I bang my head lightly. "I just keep worrying I'm going to fuck everything up and ruin our friendship for nothing. What if we only work as friends?"

"Girl, if you don't try, how are you ever going to know? You're talking crazy, like you're trying to convince yourself not to go after the man of your dreams. Why are you cockblocking yourself? Do you not think you deserve to be loved?" Her voice conveys a gentle empathy, and she covers my hand with hers as I struggle against tears again.

"Oh, Tara. I'm fucked up in all the same ways most people are. Not thinking I'm good enough, though knowing I'm way too good for Sean, for the record." I harumph as Tara's cell phone rings, and she holds up her finger to tell me she has to take this one.

She steps away and says, "Hey, boss," while I glance at my notifications. Deacon had just hearted the recent photo of me that I uploaded to my social media. My first solo photo in ten years. Comments on the photo are about my beauty, how happy they are for me to have gotten away from Sean, and how shitty he was. I'm grateful for my friends who cheerlead for me when I'm at my lowest point, and some of them have given Sean creative, endearing nicknames. "Dr. Dickweed" makes me giggle into my matcha, and I don't mind the flaming pile of dog poop GIF a college friend says reminds her of Sean.

Tara sits back down with a glum look. "I have to get to work. A situation exploded, and they need me back today instead of tomorrow. Total day-ruiner. It was great to see you. Listen, give Deacon a chance. You've spent nearly ten years with Sean's fake version of love, when the real thing is waiting. You know I'm right."

Her words ring true as we hug and say goodbye. The day is sun-drenched and a comfortable sixty-five degrees. I drive to a park near my favorite lake, kicking aside crunchy leaves to spread a comforter out beneath the shade of a giant maple, its leaves rustling in the breeze. The vast park is silent and peaceful, with only the distant lapping of waves in the lake audible. I settle in with my dog-eared dystopian romance, eager to immerse myself in a world of adventure the author has created.

I lose track of time reading and don't make my way back to Deacon's until six. When I walk in, I'm greeted by the sight of several different white Chinese food containers on the kitchen table and Deacon wolfing down his favorite Kung Pao Chicken.

"Hey!" He grins and beckons me to the table.

I flop down in the seat beside him and dig in.

I plan to act more normally around him from now on. Without meaning to, I'd been avoiding him, and he'd done nothing to deserve that. Not when he's been so good to me for so long, even opening his home to me instead of sending me back to my parents' giant mountain home. He deserves more than my distance.

It's just my overwhelming fear making me act strangely, and I'm going to get a handle on that.

"How was your day?" I ask him with a bright smile.

18

DEACON

Tuesday night, I'm standing in my mother's closet, surrounded by all her favorite things and smells, and my heart beats slowly as I stop in place and do a three hundred sixty to see the mountain of things I still have to go through.

Luckily, I have Beck with me, and she's armed with bins labeled "keep," "toss," and "give away." My first move is to go straight to my mom's jewelry safe and punch in the password —my birth date.

"Knew I was the favorite child," I tell Beck with a smirk, and she slaps my shoulder in response with a slight giggle that's music to my ears.

"Are you sure you're ready for this?" Beck asks, concerned. Her hand runs up and down my back as I let out a heavy sigh. What a loaded question. I would never be ready to spend the rest of my life without my beautiful mother, who had battled brain cancer so valiantly and eventually lost. I hate the tears that well up in my eyes, and the scratchiness of my voice as I tell her, "I'm going to try."

"It's okay if we don't get through much today. Just being

here is a big step." Beck's voice is low and soothing, and I want to walk away from this safe and into her arms, but I face forward and reach in. The little velvet bags are packed in there, containing all my mother's favorite treasures. Beck may not know it yet, but I want her to take most of them. They were willed to me and Steele after all, but Beck had been Mom's favorite.

Whenever she saw me, she'd ask how Beck was doing and if "she'd come to her senses yet." Mom had seen the wristwatch I'd bought for Beck for Christmas, and when she looked up, tears filled her eyes. "The perfect watch for the perfect girl for you, Deac, but you can't wait forever." She knew Beck's affinity for adorable watches, practically having one for every outfit, so this one had screamed her name.

I pull out a bag filled with tennis bracelets and hand them back to Beck. "Here, pick which one you'd like. There's plenty, so each of my sisters-in-law can take one too."

Beck oohs at them and tries on a bunch, asking me how each one looks, and honestly? They look right on her wrist. Mom knew in her heart Beck would be the one to end up with a lot of her jewelry when she willed it to Steele and me. After all, I've loved Beck forever, and my mother had damn well known that.

"Mom was obsessed with gemstones," I tell Beck as I find several necklaces and pass them over to Beck, who has a look of overwhelm on her pretty features.

"This is way too much," she whispers as she touches a ruby necklace gently with wide eyes.

"Oh, Beck, just wait a second. I haven't even gotten to her rings, and that's not even half of her necklaces. I'm going to leave most of those for my sisters-in-law, but there are a couple I think would be perfect for you."

I set the rings on the shelf beside the safe, and glance behind me to see Beck's eyes light up.

"Holy, holy wow." She walks up to the exact ring I knew she would. She carefully picks up the retro black diamond ring and goes completely silent.

I grab it and push it onto her left ring finger, since she's wearing the turquoise one I'd gifted her on her right. Something about the motion of placing a diamond, albeit black, on her wedding finger makes my heart skip a beat. I long to do it for real.

Beck looks up at me with tears in her eyes. "I would give this beautiful ring back in a heartbeat if it meant Lillian could still be here with us. I'd do anything, you know? I want you to know, as much as I love this ring, that it's bittersweet. This is stunning, and I love it, but it's still sad that it's not on Lillian's finger anymore. I hate that she's gone. I wanted to have Lillian as my honorary aunt."

Beck's words twist in my stomach, and I try to breathe in slowly and fully, but I'm transported back to the day she died in her hospital bed in the first-floor living room. She's telling me, "I raised an incredibly good man, Deacon. You are filled with affection and love, and I see such goodness in you. You'll make Beck a happy woman one day, and you'll be a doting daddy." Even in the end, she had faith that Beck would finally see the man standing before her for the last decade, waiting for her love.

Beck pulls me into her arms, and it's only the third time I've cried since she died three-and-a-half months ago. My shoulders shake with sobs as I stand amongst my mother's things. Beck holds me tight and whispers that it's okay to cry.

Almost as quickly as I'd let the tears come, I blink them back and yank myself away from Beck. She's an angel, and I give her a half-smile. "Thanks, Beck. Didn't expect to feel so much standing here amongst her things. It still smells like her."

"It's important to feel it. Feel it now, not later."

Sometimes I forget she's a grief counselor.

I take her hand and examine the stunning black pavé diamond on it, and before I think it through, I bend and kiss her finger right above the ring. "Yeah, this has to be yours."

Beck's eyes shine with unshed tears as she whispers, "Thank you."

"You're welcome. Take the rest of the rings, too. Oh, and I just found the turquoise earrings that go with your ring. Let me?" I walk around her and stand behind her, looking into my mother's full-length mirror. I struggle at first to find the hole in her right earlobe, but eventually I'm able to push the jewelry through and secure it.

"Holy shit." Beck touches her earlobes as I set my hands on her shoulders and peer into the mirror, meeting her eyes. A little flush makes its way to her freckled cheekbones, and I tilt my head over her shoulder and kiss her cheek.

We somehow manage to go through the entire jewelry collection in the next couple of hours. We leave many pieces for each sister-in-law, except for the rings and some wrist watches that Beck adores.

Beck goes through some of my mother's party dresses, too, and she kicks off her jeans and sweater to pull on a sparkly dress that nearly matches the turquoise ring and earring set perfectly. I don't remember ever seeing my mother wear it, but it fits Beck like a glove, and she twirls around in it with a little giggle.

"This one's cute too," I say, grabbing a navy dress that's tight to the hips and flares out. It looks like it would be fun to twirl in, and that's exactly what Beck does when she puts it on. Most of these dresses haven't even been worn yet, and I think Mom would be so happy to see Beck twirling in them.

"I feel underdressed," I chuckle.

I grab her hand and then spin her around, showing off all my best moves before I pull her to my chest, and we slow dance right there in Mom's closet. My hand on her back drifts south a bit as we dance to the music playing in our heads.

Beck laughs against my chest, burying her face in it as I prepare to dip her again. "Here we go," I whisper, extending my arm and bending her over it until her hair brushes the floor. Then, I pull her back up and into my arms.

"This is a pretty solid dance effort for no music." Beck giggles. She steps out of my arms and finds a rainbow dress with tassels, and I watch too closely as she removes the blue dress and pulls on the sequined number I don't remember my mother ever wearing. It still has tags attached.

Beck reaches for her phone and turns on her favorite Taylor Swift song.

So, I do what any self-respecting man in love would do. I spin her around, the scent of her perfume in my nose, as I sing along to the rhythm. Beck shakes her hips, the tassels on her dress a shimmering blur as she jiggles. Taylor's music vibrates through the floor as we're shaking it off. This is what Beck does for me. She takes one of the most challenging nights I can remember and fills it with vibrant warmth, music, dancing, and joy. Of course, I still miss my mother, but she'd want me to shake my ass alongside Beck in her warmly lit closet, beneath a sparkling crystal chandelier. If heaven is a thing and Mom's looking down, she's applauding.

As much as I want to kiss Beck in this moment, she pulls away laughing and clapping her hands. "That was amazing," she gushes, reaching for my hand and squeezing. "Okay if I take this dress?"

I grab one of the plastic bins and pull it over, then I work on the zipper at the back of the dress. When she steps out of it, I carefully fold it and place it in the "keep" bin, followed by the turquoise and blue ones. Beck goes through all of Mom's formal dresses and grabs about a dozen to keep, and then she finds my mother's stockpile of leggings, which are also Beck's size, and she flings handfuls of them into the keep pile.

"Are you sure you're okay with me wearing your mom's clothes? What if I look like her and it freaks you out?" Beck worries as she adds a couple of zippered sweatshirts to her haul.

"Mom would want her things to be loved and used. When you wear her clothes, all I'll think is how happy Mom would be to see you in them. So, it's fine, Beck. Really." I lean forward and stroke her cheekbone with my thumb. "It is getting late, though. How about we go through some sunglasses before we go?"

Thankfully, Dad's not home yet by the time we leave around nine. I'm unsure what to say to him now. I call and check up on him from time to time, and he talks at length about his construction company and the jobs he's raking in, but he never mentions Mom, and it's become the elephant in the room.

Just as we climb into my truck with the heavy keep bin in the backseat, Dad pulls his Tahoe in the driveway, gets out, and walks over to my open driver's window.

"Hey, son. I just wanted to be the one to tell you that I met with a realtor today. I plan on selling the house."

I scoff. "What the hell, Dad, why? This is a dream house! You and Mom built everything in there, down to arguing over the lighting and the paint colors."

Dad shakes his head sadly. "Well, it's a big place for just me, and memories of your mom are everywhere. It's time to downsize. I'll be selling most of the furniture, but if there's anything you're interested in, please let me know soon. I won't touch the closet as she willed everything in it to you and Steele, but I will have to get everything cleaned up for the listing photos."

"How much time do I have?" I ask, fighting tears that spring to my eyes.

"Two weeks before the listing agent takes photos, but you'll need to hurry and claim what you'd like so everyone else can pick from what's left."

I nod. "Got it. Okay, Dad. If this is what you need, I'll back your play."

"Hi, Aspyn," Dad greets her with a smile.

"Hey, Mr. Ambrose. Good to see you. You've been in my thoughts."

"Thanks, doll. I'm glad you're going to make use of Lillian's jewelry and clothes. That's what she would want."

"I miss her so much," Beck tells Dad. "But I want you to know her things will be well-loved."

"That's good to hear." Dad's face brightens a bit as his hand drifts up and down the side of his beard. A nervous habit, perhaps. "I've got to get inside and eat something, but you two have a good rest of your night. Deacon, feel free to text me about anything you'd like to keep for yourself, or better yet, bring over some boxes."

"I will, Dad." We shake hands through the window, and Dad walks back up the driveway to the garage.

"He's lonely," Beck realizes as she watches him leave. "Maybe we should come back tomorrow night and bring him dinner. I can make him my famous chicken pot pie."

I look over at Beck, who appears lost in thought. "That would be sweet of you, doll face."

When we get back to the house, she defrosts chicken in cool water in the sink and busies herself making enough chicken pot pie for all of us. She makes the filling separate and then announces, "I'll do the pie crusts tomorrow when I get home from work. I'm exhausted."

It's nearly eleven already, so I tell her, "Yeah, it's late, babe. You should get some rest. And you might want to take that big rock off your finger, so you don't scratch up your face tonight."

Beck walks into the living room and leans in to give me a kiss on the forehead. My heart flutters the same way it always does when her lips are anywhere near me. I say goodnight to Beck, wishing she were headed to my room so I could hold her in my arms until she falls asleep. But she takes the stairs to her bedroom, and I watch the light go out a few minutes later.

It's all right. I'm playing the long game—the really, really, *really* long game.

I click off the TV, a sigh escaping my lips when my team lost. A dull ache settles in my chest as I sink into the comfort of my bed, my sheets cool around me. They bring me no comfort. All I can think about is how much extra room I have in this king-sized bed; I long for the woman who should be curled up against my side. God, I hope there are happier times ahead. A time when Beck accepts the love I have always tried to offer her.

I imagine Dad feels a bit like I do tonight, and that's why he's chosen to sell our childhood home. A place filled with the lingering ghosts of years past instead of the sound of laughter and family. I understand it now. Houses are meant to be filled with life, not just the ache of fading memories.

The darkness pulls in around me, my breath the only sound in the room, and I whisper a little prayer for Dad— that he finds his footing in a new space, one of peace, where he can move forward. We all need that new beginning, no one more than me.

A nervous flutter goes through me as I wonder about the next steps. I know what I want, and I'm ready to step into the future, but what about Beck? How much longer would she need to heal before she's ready to admit what's always been there between us?

The following day brings a cold front and more rain, and my mood is downright gloomy. I show up to work in sweats and one of Deacon's hoodies, and I have the entire day blocked off to catch up on my client notes.

I also need to come up with an invitation for a Friends-giving at my workplace for those with nowhere else to go this coming Thanksgiving. I usually spend the holidays with Sean's family, so I don't know where I'll end up celebrating this year. I imagine Deacon will wrangle an invitation for me to his family shindig, if it's even happening this year. Lillian had always led the Thanksgiving celebration at the house, so unless one of her daughters-in-law decided to take over, the event might not happen.

My phone rings at noon, and I reach for it. "Thrive Counseling Services. This is Aspyn; how may I be of service?"

I parrot my usual line, and Mom's warm voice comes over the phone. "Hey there, honey!"

"Mom, what are you doing calling me at 4 a.m. your time?" I ask, kicking my feet up on the desk.

"My dear, menopause is full of delightful surprises like random 3 a.m. wake-up calls. While I'm up, I figure I should talk to my long-lost daughter. It's been a while, hasn't it? Which is my fault, of course." Mom easily takes the blame.

"Well, I haven't called either. I'm..." I trail off, but Mom can already hear it in my tone.

"What's the matter, darling?"

I let out a long sigh. "We broke up, Mom. A while ago, but I didn't know how to tell you. You had such high hopes for us." Tears pool in my eyes as I imagine the look of disappointment on Mom's face. "But he did some unforgivable things, and I couldn't have lived with myself if I stayed and looked like a naïve fool."

"Oh, no. What on earth happened? I thought I was leaving you in capable hands. Doctor's hands, for god's sake," Mom replies, her voice low and concerned.

"The doctor liked to put his hands on other women," is all I can think to say, and I hear Mom's gasp on the other side of the line. "Quite a few people suspected him of cheating throughout the relationship, but I didn't get any proof until the night before Tara's wedding."

"What scum!"

"Yeah." Silence descends. Words fail.

"Do you want me to come home, honey?" Mom asks after a brief quiet.

"No! Of course not, Mom, I'll be thirty soon. I can't ask you to uproot your life to comfort me after a break-up. But I'm not back at the mountain house, and I don't think I want to be in that big house all by myself, so I'm staying with Deacon in the meantime."

"He's always been such a good boy." Mom's praise sounds like she's speaking of a dog, but I'll take it. "He's a nice, responsible man. I've always liked him."

"Me too. He's good to me."

We fall silent again.

"You have feelings for him." Mom's voice lacks accusation. Her gentle intones indicate she's been in on this secret for some time. "And he has feelings for you. How's that going?"

I bite my lip until a metallic taste spreads through my mouth. I gulp. "I'm afraid. I mean, I just got out of a nearly ten-year relationship with a guy who didn't treat me well, who controlled me and was abusive in some ways."

"Abusive?" Mom asks.

"In some ways," I nearly whisper. "And now he's gone and gotten his mistress pregnant. So, he'll be a dad before I ever get the chance to be a mother, like I've always wanted. And I know he doesn't want it. Doesn't deserve it. No child should be the child of a narcissist, and in the end, that's all Sean was. A very good one. He fooled everyone."

Mom weeps quietly on the other side of the phone, and I resent that I have to worry about her feelings right now, instead of my own.

I'm surprised when she says, "Oh, Aspyn. I feel so guilty for thinking he was the perfect man for you because he had goals. He is a doctor and he comes from a good family. I thought you'd won the lottery with him, and I hate that I didn't see through him. I pushed you onto him, told you so many times to forgive him. I gave him the benefit of the doubt when I should have listened to you instead."

"It's not your fault. You saw what he showed you; that's what a narcissist does, Mom. They're charming until they've enchanted you, and once they have you, they break you down in every way until you're dependent on them. Constantly manipulating you with their lies and falsehoods, making you believe you're crazy every time you doubt them or are critical of them. They erode your trust in yourself. Without seeing the messages between him and the other woman, I probably would have married him and had his babies, and..." I sigh. "And it would have all continued. Because he chipped away at my self-worth and made me think I didn't deserve better."

Mom blows out a breath. "I'm so sorry." Her simple, unqualified words mean so much. She finally adds, "I love you, daughter."

I smile a little. "I love you, too. And listen, don't blame yourself. Sean is an effective liar. I'm embarrassed, as someone in the mental health field, that I didn't see it sooner. But sometimes when you're in something, you're too deep to see the big picture. In the end, Sean did me a favor by leaving his Kindle charging in the kitchen and clueing me in to all his deceptions. I am much happier now that he's gone. I'm in a good place to rebuild."

"You've got Deacon. You're going to be okay, baby. Lean on him if you need to, and on your friends, as well. You have excellent friends."

I smile. "You're right. I do. And they rallied around me. Even Tara wants to stay friends despite the breakup. She's disgusted with Sean, too. Her wedding was beautiful. I wish you had been able to come."

"Me too, honey. I know she and Cody are going to be happy together for a long time." I can hear her smile through the phone. "And you two are as close as sisters. I'm glad she isn't letting the breakup come between you."

I let out a little sigh. "Thanks for calling, Mom. I have a lot to do today before I go over to Deacon's dad's place and help him go through her things. His dad is going to sell the place, and we only have two weeks to go through it. So, I'm taking dinner over there and going through what I can with Deacon tonight."

"He's lucky to have a friend like you. I sure do miss Lillian."

I try not to mention how she'd missed her funeral. I'm still a little bitter about that.

"Me too. Every day." I bite my lip and sigh. "Well, I have to go. Let Daddy know I'm doing just fine. Things work out the way they're meant to, right?"

"Always. We'll talk soon." Mom disconnects the line, and I set my phone down in its cradle.

Things *do* work out. I'm not pregnant and anchored to Sean for the rest of my days. And Deacon and I have each other, no matter how complicated the unspoken feelings are that lie between us.

❧

LATER THAT NIGHT, TOM'S NOT HOME, SO I LEAVE THE chicken pot pie in his fridge and join Deacon in the same closet we'd spent the evening before. He gathers a couple of quilts his grandmother made and puts them in the "keep" bin, along with a photo album of Deacon from his youth. We've found many sentimental items and resisted going through them, since Deacon seems to be in a pensive mood, lost in his own thoughts.

"Do you know what tomorrow is?" Deacon asks as I try on a black romper of Lillian's.

"Thursday?"

"Other than that? I mean, in history?"

I think back and come up empty. "Nope. Just a regular Thursday, I imagine?"

"It's the tenth anniversary of the frat party. The first night we met," Deacon tells me, his voice low as he sits in a corner going through a box of photos.

Holy shit. So, it is. It would be the tenth anniversary of my first kiss with Sean, and the night I met Deacon. The night, in hindsight, I wish had gone so differently.

I gulp. "I wish I could rewind ten years and make some very different decisions."

Deacon doesn't answer, just pulls out a photo and grins. "Mom took this photo of us. This is at Christmas, nine years ago." He hands it to me, and I glance down at the image I've never seen before. I'm wearing a gold fringe dress that reminds me of a Taylor Swift video, with my hair dyed blonde in curled ringlets, and Deacon stands a few inches from me, wearing a khaki suit. We look color-coded, but we hadn't planned it that way. Even our hair is similarly honey colored.

"Wow. This was so long ago—my first Christmas party with the Wrights. I wasn't even close with Tara yet, but your mother made me feel right at ease. She took me under her wing and introduced me to everyone. Thank goodness for Lillian." I smile up at Deacon. "Look how we're dressed. Like we planned it ahead of time!"

"Sean was irritated about that, too." Deacon rolls his eyes, though I don't remember Sean's reaction to it. "He didn't let on, but he tried to keep us from each other that night. We were on the front porch talking philosophy, and he couldn't have dragged you away faster."

My lips quirk up. "So many red flags I ignored."

"Neon ones," Deacon adds as he puts the photo into a hat box along with others he plans to keep. "That one's getting framed. Oh, here's another. Look how cute you were, fast asleep."

He hands it over, and I smile down at the image of me asleep in Deacon's lap on a couch, my hair splayed all around him. The back of the photo states it was about five years earlier.

"Drunk on ginger beer," I recall. "And sick to my stomach from too many chocolate-covered cherries."

Deacon laughs. "Those were expensive. I got them for you

when I had to travel to Denver a couple of days before Christmas."

"You were the one who got them for me? I think Sean took the credit." I roll my eyes as I hand the picture back.

"That's what Sean was good at. Not showing any thoughtfulness and stealing the credit." Deacon harrumphs and then adds, "And yes to the black romper. It's adorable."

I add it to the growing keep container as I hear the rain pitter-patter on the roof above us. It's been coming down steadily all day long, but at least it's not snow. Yet. Though, at least in the snow, there was fun to be had on snowmobiles, skis, and going ice fishing.

"Winter's just around the bend," Deacon says as if he were reading my mind. "You should go through my mom's coats in the front hall closet. She has a plum-colored peacoat that would look stunning on you."

I turn on my heel and follow his directions, staring at many adorable scarves I find hanging inside the closet. Her Chanel peacoat fits me perfectly, so I grab a few scarves and take the coats back up to the closet.

Deacon is sitting on the floor with his shoulder shaking, and my heart constricts. I drop the items, kneel between his legs awkwardly, and pull him into my arms. His wet face rests on my neck as he continues to cry, his shoulders heaving.

"Let it out," I encourage him, my hand in his messy blond waves as I hold him tight. His hands tangle in my hair as he tugs me even closer. "It's okay, Deacon. You're going to be okay."

"I can't believe this house is going to belong to someone else," Deacon manages through his sobs.

"I know it hurts, honey, and it's okay to feel that. But hopefully, someone buys it and can fill it up with all the love this house has seen from your family over the years. And your dad can find something smaller that fits him just right without daily reminders of everything he's lost. That's what he needs to do to cope."

Deac nods and sniffles, pulling back to stare into my eyes. "I never thought I'd lose Mom like that. Nine months, you know? Then, poof. Gone."

Tears course down his cheeks, and I wipe them away with my fingertips. I slide my hand through his golden locks and inch forward, bringing my lips to his tears as I kiss them away tenderly.

"They told us six months to three years. Why couldn't it have been three years?" Deacon cries angrily. "There's so much I wish she could be here for."

"It wasn't fair. It never is." I wipe his tears. "But you have to believe she's looking down from somewhere peaceful, proud of the way you've been living your life, Deacon." I mop up the area beneath his eyes. I notice the dark circles and wonder if he's been having trouble sleeping. "And please, Deac, let me be here for you. I'm strong enough to shoulder some of your grief. To hold it for you, so you can set it down once in a while."

Deacon nods and dries his tears. "You know, I have to believe, long after we're dead and gone, there's somewhere we'll all be together again after this is over. That love is an eternal bond that will let us find each other again." Deacon clasps my hands in his and lets me see the depth of his grief for Lillian.

Kneeling, I press my chest to his, and I stare into his ocean eyes. "Then, there is. There's a wonderful place where nothing ever ends, nothing is so painfully temporary, and there's no more loss. Somewhere meant for reunions. If you believe it, I believe it."

He wraps his arms around me and whispers, "I like to think she tap-danced her way to what's waiting for all of us after."

I smile, remembering his mother's affinity for dance, and I picture it in my head—her dancing away as the curtain closed on her final performance.

I burst into tears, and then we're both blubbering messes, clutching one another and feeling our collective loss deeply in a closet that still smells like Lillian's perfume.

Thursday, I take off work. It's nice working for yourself and setting your hours, for moments like these. My receptionist slash assistant knows I'll be gone, so she puts out any of the little fires that arise throughout the day.

Meanwhile, I turn my bedroom and bathroom into the rose section of my local grocer, placing soft, velvety petals in a heart design on the bed and creating a fragrant aisle on the ground that leads to the bedroom. I know I'm being overly hopeful, but I feel closer than ever to Beck after we'd held each other, and she'd kissed away my tears in my mother's bedroom last night.

It's been a month since Sean and Beck ended their relationship. Maybe I'm an optimist thinking Beck is closer to being ready to consider me now. Every day is agonizing, trying to keep my hands to myself when she lives under my roof and steals my hoodies every night. I want to give her time, but I don't want to waste it. Life is never promised; I learned that when my mother took her last breath, still so young and vibrant. Is it wrong of me to remind Beck what we could have had if only that day ten years ago had gone differently?

When Beck gets home, I miss my opportunity because she runs up the stairs with a bag in her hands and tells me, "I'll be down in a bit!"

I sit on the couch for an hour, lost in thought. Why had Beck pulled away from me over the last weeks? I try to trace my memories back to the moment it happened.

That's when it hits me. It's so obvious, I feel like an absolute idiot.

Beck must have overheard at least part of my argument with Sean. She had to have, because it's the only thing that explains both her momentary lapses of letting me too close, and the other moments of pushing me away.

Beck's probably pondering her own feelings or lack thereof, and if she does have feelings for me, she's terrified of them.

Shit. What's the right move here? Not for me; for Beck. She lost Sean after putting up with his bullshit for so long, expecting a ring that never came. Her heart's been obliterated by his pattern of cheating, and now she's probably heard how Sean called dibs on her the night we spotted her. Maybe she hates me for letting his "dibs" go unchallenged. I know I hate myself for it every single day, and I imagine all the ways things could have gone differently. Even Beck told me she wishes she could rewind and change things.

Maybe we can.

Suddenly, Beck appears at the top of the steps and asks, "What do you think?"

When I turn on the overhead lights, I spot her standing with her hands on her hips in a two-piece, white-and-gray-striped nightgown, her once golden hair now the same shade of pink it had been when I'd first seen her behind the punch bowl on that fateful night.

I'm stunned—she's stunning. She looks every bit as angelic as she did the night we met, when I was too much of a pussy to tell Sean to eat shit. If I'd had even the slightest knowledge of who Beck was at the time, I would have trampled over Sean's body to get to her first. There's nothing I won't do for Beck. I just have to hope she's amenable to what comes next.

"Come here," I demand, standing up and meeting her at the bottom of the steps.

I let out a deep breath, anxiety taking hold of me. "Hi there...I just wanted to tell you that you're beautiful. I really love your pink hair. My name is Deacon. This is my frat house. Would you like a margarita?"

Her eyes soften, and a smile eases across her face. "Hey, I'm Aspyn Beckett, but my best friend in the world calls me Beck. I'd love a margarita. This punch sucks. I think there's Red Bull in it. Who does that?" Beck's nose wrinkles, and I reach out for her hand, which she gives me. "You don't have a skeezy dark-haired friend here that's about to give me some cheap line about my clothes looking better on his floor, do you?"

"Friend? Who? I don't see anyone here. It's just us." I look around the room exaggeratedly and ask, "Is it your first frat party?"

"Yes. I came with my roommate, but I think she's sucking face with some block-headed football player, and I just transferred here, so I have no idea how to get back to my dorm from here."

"Then, let's have a margarita, and then I'll walk you back and get you home safe. So, what's your major?" I hold both her hands in mine and stare into her eyes, feeling a deep vulnerability.

"Psychology. I love to figure out how people work, what they want, and what makes them tick. I like to think I've got a hidden talent for mind-reading. Do you want me to read yours?" Beck asks.

I chuckle. "I should say no. I'm just a nineteen-year-old frat boy with no idea what I plan on doing with my life. Right now, I think I'm going to be a lead singer in a hit band. Pop with heavy synth. My band breaks up after a two-week tour, though I don't know that yet."

"You'll figure out what you're meant to do. And as for the mind-reading, it's simple. You think I look like a fucking angel beneath these twinkly lights," Beck whispers, stepping closer to my chest as she places her hands flat on it. "And you love my pink hair. See, mind reading."

Beck confirms my suspicion. She heard everything I told Sean the night of the barbecue. My face heats under her wide-eyed stare.

"I just told some asshole to get lost. He tried to call dibs on the most beautiful girl in the place. He would have been all wrong for you," I say quietly, still playing along as we replay the night we met, exactly the way it should have gone down. I train my eyes on her luscious, pale pink lips. "And I know that you've been hurt before, and since we've just met, this is a big leap. But I'd like to touch that gorgeous hair and taste your lips, Aspyn Beckett. Before the night's over."

I reach out and run my hand through her damp but soft hair, and her eyes seem to dilate as they fix on mine.

"Why wait? I've been waiting nineteen years for my first kiss, and now seems as good a time as any," Beck whispers as she tiptoes and presses the entirety of her chest against mine, her arms encircling my neck.

I tilt my face towards hers, and Beck's eyes look like a green blaze, bright and sparkling. I back up a few steps, the rough plaster of the wall pressing against my back as I finally stop. Beck follows me step for step, until she presses her body against mine. Her tongue darts out, and she sexily licks her lower lip.

"I'm going to take my time with you, Beck," I whisper to both versions of Beck: both nineteen and twenty-nine. "Savor the way you feel as I slide my hands up your shirt to your waist..." The whisper-soft brush of my fingers against the cotton of her pajamas sends electricity through my fingertips. She's got to feel it buzzing through her skin.

My hands settle on her warm, slim waist, skin smooth and soft against my fingertips.

"And I'll kiss you slowly, taste your delectable skin," I demonstrate, the feather-light touch of my lips on her temple, her forehead, then a playful brush against the tip of her nose. Beck grins, a flash of straight, white teeth, as I playfully nibble her nose. I rain down a cascade of kisses on her chin and jawline as my hand slides under her shirt. I hold her close, the scent of her strawberry-scented soap filling the air. The night we met blends seamlessly into this October Thursday, both nights merging into a straightforward desire: Beck.

Her fingers cup my cheeks, pulling my face toward hers. Her minty breath fills my nostrils as her hazel eyes flutter shut, her lips parting. My mouth finds hers, and it's filled with aching tenderness and desperate need. Her kiss is soft yet urgent, and her hand clenches the fabric of my blue Henley as I open my mouth to hers. Quiet desperation hums between us, and then Beck's soft, smooth tongue darts out and seeks mine, a taste of longing fulfilled after ten years of waiting.

"I hear you're the one who wants to stay forever," Beck whispers as she pulls back to catch her breath, her hands up in my hair, which she tugs between her fingers, my body buzzing with need for hers.

"If you give me this one chance, that's a promise I'm ready to make. I'll call dibs on the rest of your life," I promise her, my heart hammering in my chest as she looks up at me with vulnerability and adoration.

Thank god. Thank god my pink-haired Beck is back. The girl she was back then was anything but shy; she was confident, alluring, and whip smart. That was before Sean picked her apart for ten years. But as she stands in front of me, waiting for our next hot kiss, I know that girl isn't too far gone.

"You've been holding on to that since the night of the barbecue, letting me think you hadn't heard. No wonder you've been acting so strangely after hearing my confessions. I wanted to give you time, Beck, but I will if you need me to. What should I do here?"

"Kiss me again," she whimpers.

A wave of heat washes over me. I bend, capturing Beck's lips in a possessive brand. My teeth graze her lower lip, biting gently, a sharp contrast to the soft, soothing kisses I give her afterward. Her fingers, always chilly, seek the warmth of my chest beneath my shirt, and she makes a playful dance to my pectoral muscles and back again, sending shivers down my spine.

I want her so bad it hurts.

Beck pulls back and whispers, "I'm only nineteen. I'm so new at this stuff. Honestly, I should tell you goodnight, let you walk me home."

But her hazel eyes smolder with desire, and I'm not sure if I should play along with this one or challenge her.

"You belong with me, Beck," I tell her honestly. "Bring your pillows. Your smutty books. Your bedside lip balm and night moisturizer. Come to my room tonight. Live with me for real."

"Okay. And hey, I also read fiction." She rolls her eyes and adds, "Give a girl a few minutes. I have loads of stuff. What kind of thread count are your sheets sporting?" Her eyes narrow like there's a very definitive bar set, and I don't want to fail.

"A thousand. They're antimicrobial with silver in them, and they're clean, crisp, and ready to smell like you." I cup her cheek. "Now, go get your things, Beck. I've been sleeping alone for too long and so have you."

I get to work cleaning out the bedside table on her side.

She manages to tear herself away from me, runs back up the stairs, and then calls me up. She places an armful of pillows, tops it with her satiny purple robe, and a pair of matching plush slippers. Meanwhile, she's loaded up a canvas bin full of books, face and hair products, supplements, and even a toothbrush.

When we get to my room, I tell her, "This is your home too, Beck." She notices the roses immediately. She sets her bin down on my bed, picks up a handful of roses, and releases them over her head as she twirls.

"So romantic. And this is the only place I want to be. Here with you," she practically hums. "I suppose you thought you were getting lucky tonight, huh?"

"I had hope." I flash her a grin.

"Give me just a minute to put these things away, babe," she tells me as she unloads her things and arranges them quickly on the bedside table.

I notice the books on top in a stack.

"Mmm, I don't think there's one fiction book amongst these." I glance at the titles. "Hockey romance. Dark romance. Romantasy. Best friend's father. More hockey."

Grabbing one, I flip open to page fifty-nine, and I get the gist immediately. "This one is interesting. He's set to marry this girl's sister, but when she doesn't show up, this girl takes her sister's place. Only they've secretly been in love since they were children. I'm sure this is steamy as hell."

I turn the page. Boom. There's the sex.

"I'm not sure how a cock quivers, but this is some filthy shit, my saucy little minx," I tell Beck, who grabs a pillow and chucks it at my head.

"I love my filth, thank you very much." Beck smacks my arm and removes the book from my hands. "But I'm also not sure how his member quivers. Can't picture it. Either way, the smut works and has kept me company on many lonely nights."

"No more of those for you," I tell her.

"Good. Wow, I love this fireplace," Beck tells me, leaving the bedside and walking over to the two-sided fireplace to the left of the bed, which separates the room from the adjoining bathroom. A giant soaking tub sits on the other side, and I can picture Beck there in the winter, submersed in bubbles, reading her filthy books.

"You'll adore the tub. It's deep enough to cover my whole body, and the fireplace puts out great heat," I tell her. We have beautiful but short autumns, and we're no stranger to early snowfalls. The fluffy white stuff is expected to arrive by the end of this month. "Let me flip it on now. It's only forty-five degrees tonight, and your fingers are cold."

I click a button to turn on the fire, and it roars to life, making shadows dance along the walls. I light a few candles and turn out the lights before I take a handful of rose petals and dump them over her head.

Then, Beck grabs me by the Henley and tugs me to her, melting her mouth into mine for another sweet kiss. "Thank you for the roses."

"Anything for you, Beck," I whisper before I slide my tongue into her willing mouth and savor the way she tastes. Her eyes fill with tears, and she gives me a nod filled with acceptance and bravery. She's taking the next step. Beck climbs up on the bed, and I get a great view of her backside as she crawls to the top and slides beneath the sheet and comforter. With a happy sigh, Beck leans back against her pillows that have taken over the bed.

"Jesus, Beck. You're in my bed." I can't believe my luck as she lies there, her arms above her head, stretching out comfortably. "I mean, you were in my bed once before, and I wanted to touch you, but I knew you were just lonely. I didn't want to cross lines that night."

Beck snorts with an eye roll. "The next morning was when I realized my feelings for you. It was so hard not to beg you to touch me. I woke up with your hard dick against my ass, and I wanted to get on top of you and fuck you senseless."

The confession stuns me. My mouth drops open, astounded to hear her dirty thoughts about me.

"But I just ran to my room and got myself off quick, because it was moving day." Beck gives me a sexy wink.

I groan. "Oh, to be a fly on that wall...Beck, the thought of you fingering yourself makes me want to explode."

She gives me a sexy grin. "Oh yeah? Well, what we're going to do next is going to make you spontaneously combust, then. You ready?"

�֎ 21 ֍

ASPYN

"**O**h, I'm more than ready," Deacon tells me. "Ten years in the making."

I return his warm smile, and our mouths meet, electricity crackling between us as we melt into each other.

"Some things are worth the wait," I whisper.

The place between my thighs pulses with desire as he rubs a hand from my ankle up to the inside of my knee. I bend the knee back until the outside of it hits the blanket, scattering the roses that cover my most intimate area, unveiling me.

"Are you ready?" Deacon looks to me for permission, and I give a single nod, surprising myself with how certain I am so soon. I've never been readier for anything, despite how quickly we've moved.

He pushes my thighs apart and kisses up the insides of my legs, tickling my skin as he goes. Rose petals fall off me as I arch my back. When he slides his open mouth from the inner thigh to my center and strokes his tongue against me, I gasp, feeling heat course through my veins as he reaches up for my hips and holds me tightly in place.

"So delicious. Mmm," Deacon groans, lapping at me with

his tongue in earnest, both of us moaning as he finds the long-neglected parts of me that drive me to madness.

When his tongue licks up to my clit, I screech and press my hips up firmly against his face. Reading my not-so-subtle signs, he circles it with his tongue and then sucks the tiny bud into his mouth hard until I begin to exhale loudly and gasp at uneven intervals, feeling my world tilting on its axis as I reach for his hair and marvel at the fact that this is finally happening. This intimacy is something I'll reserve for Deacon for the rest of my life. I can't imagine anyone else ever licking me this way or touching me like this, or wanting to be with anyone else.

"Come for me, Beck. I can tell you're close. Be a good girl and let me hear you," Deacon whispers against my skin as he strokes my clit with his thumb and spears me deep with his tongue, over and over again as I writhe, undone by the plea-sure that comes close to approaching agony. Everything throbs, including my heart, as I glance down at him between my legs, looking so sexy. So mine.

"Deacon, yes!" I cry, as my stomach muscles twist painfully, and my knees go weak. I press myself firmly against his tongue as my body begins to quake for him. Then, all I hear are broken cries as I shatter, falling over the edge into a powerful orgasm. I'm sobbing for Deacon as I pulse around his tongue. My entire body spasms, out of my control, but that's okay because Deacon is in charge, and I'm happy to let him be.

I come down quietly, trying to catch my breath, as Deacon slips onto the bed beside me, pulls my back to his chest, and captures my legs with his. We're twisted up together when he whispers, "You came so hard for me. Did you hear how loud you screamed?"

"I heard. Think I hurt my own ears. I can't believe how

long I've waited for that! How good it feels to be with you this way."

"You taste incredible, and you're so gorgeous and pink, like these gorgeous nipples. God, you're responsive. I love your sighs," Deacon tells me reverently, his sexy words making me bite my lower lip, hard. He reaches around me and bravely explores my nipples. "So delicious. Don't think I'm done with you. I'm just giving you a breather." He reaches around me and brazenly explores my nipples. I gasp, my hips lurching back toward his in response. Deacon chuckles. He's having way too much fun torturing me, so I circle my hips and rub my ass against his hardness to tease him.

He drops his hand down and lightly strokes my sex as I shiver.

"It's definitely me quivering, not your cock," I tell him as my head falls back against his chest, remembering the word from my smutty book.

"I can feel you throb against my fingers. I can't believe I get to touch you this way. I've waited so long, baby. You have no idea how long I've wanted this, to own your body this way." Deacon drags his fingertip across my clit and just holds it there while I make a desperate noise in my throat, pushing firmly against his hand. *Please*, I beg internally. "And you're impossible to satisfy, huh? I make you come, and you're desperate for more?"

"Desperate for only you," I whisper. "I'll never get enough of you, Deac. But it's your turn to let me love you. Here." I toss a pillow on the ground and kneel with my mouth open, and Deacon gets the picture. He's so sexy as he walks toward me, leans back against the edge of the bed and says, "God, you look so beautiful on your knees for me. Now, open wider."

I obey, and he shoves his thick length into my throat in one quick slide.

"Oh, fuck, doll face," Deacon whimpers. "Look at you taking me so well. What a good girl you are for me." His fingertips stroke my cheeks and lips as I take him deep, managing to swallow almost all of him before I release him and do it again, licking his sensitive underside as I take him inch by inch until he's fully buried. I feel so sexy doing this thing I used to hate. Lucky, even, knowing the man attached to this cock absolutely loves and adores me. He moves his hands through my hair tenderly. When his hips move, my eyes water, and I release him again to gasp for breath.

"Fuck, honey," Deacon whispers to me as he bends to kiss me deeply, shoving his tongue into my mouth. "I love the way I feel in your throat."

"Then don't stop," I tell him, directing his cock back where we both want it. I moan around him, vibrating him with my throat as I work to get him even deeper. My sex throbs with desire as I gag and suck, eager to welcome him into my body.

"Where do you want me to come?" Deacon groans.

"Inside of me. I need you." It's a soft plea falling from my lips, which he kisses. "Give me you."

"This was inevitable, baby. You and me. And we're forever." Deacon's eyes search mine, and his expression becomes desperate.

I push to stand and trace his shoulder with my fingertips, pressing a kiss to the side of his neck. "I love you, Deac. Make me yours." My voice holds a dare.

"I love you too," he whispers, kissing me before he throws me on the bed, covering my breasts in open-mouthed kisses, bringing his fingers to my wet center and sliding inside while he licks my nipple. I convulse, my breath becoming gasps, and then he perches between my legs and sucks my clit. My heart soars to some other realm as my hands fist in his hair as I lose control. I'm a second from coming when his body covers mine and he thrusts into my dripping core. The world darkens and becomes so small that it's only the two of us. Nothing else matters or exists at all but the blinding pleasure that courses through me, and how well we fit together, like I'm a puzzle that's found its missing piece at last.

He thrusts again, burying the entirety of his length inside me until he's totally sheathed. It takes me a second to adjust to his thickness, but goddamn, am I a lucky woman to be with someone as amazing as Deacon. He's my whole world as he bottoms out and waits for the ache to lessen. It only takes a few seconds until pure need flows through me, and I wrap my legs around his waist and tilt my hips to take him deeper.

"Hard," I beg.

With every thrust of Deacon's powerful hips, he finds a spot in me that makes me gasp and squeeze my eyes shut, pleasure surging through my veins until I'm hardly rooted to reality. I'm just Deacon's, living for every press of him against *that* spot.

"Just like that, Deac," I whimper, my voice thick with need.

Deacon hits the right spot again and again until all coherent thoughts leave my head and there is only feeling.

"You like that?"

"God, yes," I whine between pants and then move his hand to my breasts where I need his touch.

A sob rises out of the depths of me. This connection between us is the sexiest thing I've ever experienced. My heart is in his hands. I want to stay joined like this forever, but I know Deacon's getting close. His hands leave my nipples and reach around my ass as he lifts my hips and slides more easily in and out of me, pistoning himself fast as I mumble in delirious pleasure. My heart rate spirals out of control as I give everything in me, every part of me, over to this man, trusting him entirely.

When Deacon gives one last powerful thrust and spurts deep inside of me, I scream out, too. We come together, my body giving in to the sensations racing through me without hesitation. His hand rubs my clit, expertly prolonging my orgasm, stretching out the bliss over minutes instead of seconds, while my body spasms and tightens everywhere. I close my eyes and hold on through the waves of pleasure that ripple through me ceaselessly until I'm limp. Deacon is groaning, "Fuck, fuck, fuck," as he gives a few last thrusts, neither of us eager to be finished with our first time.

Deacon finally flips off me, tugs me to his side, and holds me until I stop shaking. I tuck my face against his neck, my breathing still uneven.

All I can think is, *holy shit, that was so intense.* I marvel at the fact that, this whole time, I haven't thought of Sean once.

I glance over at Deac's face as he lies resting with his eyes closed, wearing an unmistakable look of joy that matches how I feel. His eyes crinkle around the corners, and all I can think to do is inch up and kiss him all over his face, including his little smile lines.

"I feel so lucky to have you, baby." I voice the only thought that runs through my mind before I press my mouth to his in the gentlest of kisses.

"No, Beck. I'm the luckiest."

✿ 22 ✿

DEACON

It's nearly November, and the winter dreariness has set in, so I'm cuddled up in bed early with the fireplace blazing, Beck reading one of her naughty books next to me. If I'm lucky, she'll feel like reenacting a scene from one of them.

My brother Steele calls me to congratulate me on "finally winning Aspyn's heart," which he'd heard through "the grapevine." I hadn't been the one to tell him. Frankly, I've been so wrapped up being in love with Beck that I've hardly talked to my family much lately. I'm far too occupied with having my dream girl to keep anything else on my radar right now. I should feel guilty, but I don't.

"Listen, I have a bunch of boxes of your old things I helped Dad clean out of the basement. Books, mementos, Spiderman sheet sets, the whole nine. How about I bring them by tomorrow afternoon?"

"That would be great."

"I also took the jewelry safe from the closet. You mentioned that Aspyn took a lot of the jewelry, like we know

Mom intended, so maybe she can use the safe for those pieces?" Steele suggests.

"Sure. Sounds great, bro. Did the sisters-in-law go through the rest of the jewelry, sunglasses, hats, and everything else?" I reach over and kiss Beck's cheek while she's immersed in her book, and she pushes my face away with a giggle.

I do manage to wrench her from the book eventually, after I pluck it from her hands and read a very sexy scene aloud. Then, Beck jumps my bones, and I enjoy every second of it.

❦

THE NEXT DAY, STEELE ARRIVES BY 4 P.M. WITH BOXES upon boxes, which we haul up to the primary bedroom. Beck sits on the bed, telling us she'll "oversee" the operation.

Now, I'm standing in the middle of the room, looking around at all the boxes, a bit bewildered. Steele throws himself into the recliner in the sitting area portion of the bedroom and yawns like he's just hiked a mountain.

"Big job," Steele tells me, arching a well-manicured brow at me, making the understatement of the year. I put my hands on my hips and sighed.

"How does Dad seem to you?" I ask Steele as I open a duct-taped box full of thrillers.

"Like a man who lost his wife way too soon and isn't ready to face his grief." Steele sighs.

"Fuck." I'd gotten the same feeling. "Any offers on the house? I know he just put it on the market Tuesday."

"They're starting the showings today, which is why I hauled all this shit away for him a couple days ago. He said he had a long way to go on the house and was hiring a cleaning team. Made me feel bad. I had to work Thursday and Friday, or I would have done it for him."

"I could've helped," Beck speaks up, sounding disappointed not to have been asked. "If Tom ever needs something, I'm here. Please remember that."

"Thanks, Aspyn. He seemed resolute about the cleaning team, so I didn't try to change his game plan. Anyway, I'm sure the offers will roll in despite it being winter. The major snow hasn't started yet, and Dad has offered a quick closing. I guess the house he wants is vacant, and they will allow a quick close, too."

"He's already found a new place?" Beck asks, drumming her fingernails along her hardback book.

"Yeah, in a fifty-five and up community not too far from here. He'll be even closer to you and me, Deac." Steele kicks his feet up on the recliner.

"We'll have to have him over to dinner when he gets settled," Beck decides sweetly. "Your dad probably needs us now more than ever. It helps to keep busy."

"He's working a lot. Keeping himself busy to distract from the grief, I'm sure," I tell my brother and Beck.

"That sounds about right," Aspyn agrees. When silence stretches out between us, she asks, "So, Steele, what's been happening with you? Will you be bringing a girlfriend home anytime soon? Popping out some babies?" Beck gives him a half-smile as she quizzes him.

He gives his usual answer.

"I've got thirty babies at school. Currently, no prospects, and I'm so busy, I hardly have time to meet anyone. But don't worry about me."

"You're not getting any younger, Mr. Thirty-One-Year-Old," Beck teases him. "Sorry, I hate that line. It's what people asked me all the time about my relationship with Sean. 'Where are you and Sean going?' Well, hopefully the only place he's going is hell."

"I think everyone should wait until they're truly ready anyway. I'm only a year older than Deac, and I don't see a wedding ring on your finger or hear any babies crying." Steele teases Beck right back.

I smile and reply, "Funny how those are the exact things I want." I shoot Steele a smile.

"Heard. This is me swooning." Beck places the back of her hand on her forehead and tilts her head back in a mock-swoon and then winks at me.

"Not telling you anything you don't already know, love." I get up and walk over to her, kissing her deeply right in front of Steele, who immediately covers his eyes but peeks through two fingers jokingly. Beck giggles against my lips.

Beside me sits my mother's giant jewelry box, which she'd placed inside her closet safe.

"Ooh, I have lots of jewelry to fill that with." Beck's eyes open wide, and she walks over to the top drawer of her dresser, which we'd recently moved out of storage and into the primary bedroom. The top drawer is lined in velvet, but we'd both prefer if the expensive items stay in the safe.

"I love this ring so much." Beck takes out the black cushion-cut diamond, and her eyes shine as she stares at it.

"It's stunning on you, baby," I tell her. "And it's sized right?"

"Like it was made for me." Beck grins. She takes it off her finger and hands it to me. I suddenly know I'm going to use this ring to propose that we start our lives together.

"You're sure that's the one you want?" I ask, my heart thumping in my chest until Beck nods and shares a secret smile that tells me we're on the same page. I bring my mouth to hers and taste her lips.

"That's part of a set," Steele says, getting up out of the recliner and digging in the jewelry box. "You must have missed it. Look. It's a band with black diamonds and rubies all around it. These came together. I remember the day Mom got them."

Beck's eyes are wide as saucers, nearly popping out of her skull, as she spots the band Steele is holding out. I steal it from him, along with the black diamond ring. They shimmer brilliantly as I hold them up to the light, much flashier than Beck's usual turquoise, but if she says it's the one, then it is.

When Beck turns back to talk to Steele, I slip it carefully into my pocket with my heart thrumming in my chest.

If that's the ring my girl wants to wear, then that's what she'll wear for the rest of her life.

I've got a plan.

✿ 23 ✿

ASPYN

As the gloomy November days pass, there's a day when Deacon is suspiciously out of contact with me. I message him but get no response for most of the afternoon. Nervously and compulsively checking my texts, I finally throw my phone against the couch and give up by around 4 p.m.

While I trust Deacon, I spent ten years with a pathological liar, so I can't help but confront him when he arrives in time for dinner.

"Where were you today?" I try to sound casual, but Deacon looks up and meets my eyes with a slightly hurt expression, a frown on his face.

"My love, I was busy putting together a surprise for you for tomorrow. All I need is for you to trust me and let me pack an overnight bag for you. You'll want to dress for the weather. We'll leave around three-thirty, all right?" Deacon's gentle voice reminds me that he's trustworthy, and my hang-ups are the reason I've made this an issue. Come to think of it, it may be time to return to therapy. I don't want to bring my insecurities from my last relationship into forever, which is how long I intend to spend with Deacon.

"I'm sorry about that. I didn't mean to doubt you, Deac. I love you, and of course, you can pack a bag for me." I smile at him, and he finally sends me one in return, relief etched in his expression as he flops back in his chair and lets out a breath.

THE NEXT DAY, I OBSESS, TRYING TO FIGURE OUT WHAT MY big surprise is. I also struggle to find the perfect outfit for it. All Deacon tells me is to dress warmly, so I pick out a soft, pink-ribbed sweater with a plunging neckline, a matching Burberry scarf, and a linen-blend, wide-legged pair of jeans with flat leather booties in a soft brown. Now that my hair is pink again, I'm embracing my former favorite color.

I've spent too much time on my hair, nails, and makeup by the time Deacon walks in from work at 3 p.m.

He walks toward me, drops his briefcase, and asks, "Is that red lipstick going to get all over my face when I kiss you, baby?"

I grin. "It's Color Stay."

With that, he takes my lips with his and kisses me hard, shoving his tongue past my teeth until our tongues duel. Deacon presses me back against the nearest wall and slides his hands up my belly until he gains access to my breasts and begins to pinch my nipples as the kiss turns hot and desperate.

Finally, he pulls back, wipes a hand over his face, and groans. "If we keep this up, you'll be late to your surprise. Let me just get changed. Just remember where we left off so we can pick this up again later, will ya?"

I give him an exaggerated wink. "I was just going to get on my knees for you. I'll remember."

Desire surges through me, and I try to tame it. I've also spent all day trying not to look in the overnight bag that Deacon packed for me last night for any clues about where we're going. He's packed his fancy camera, that much I know, and he comes downstairs after changing into dark jeans and a dark gray sweater with a few pillows and our overnight bags.

"Everything else is ready for us," Deacon announces. "You got everything you need? Floss? Your fancy face cream? That watermelon lip balm you love so much?"

"Got it all."

"Face mask? Earplugs in case I snore?" Deacon asks.

"One sec!" I run back and grab my face mask, which is all black and in glitter, and it says, "Fuck Off." I grab a cozy throw blanket off the bed and then I head back downstairs with a smile.

I'm ready for the surprise.

Before we leave, Deacon slips a little key into my palm and whispers, "Keep that safe."

He makes me put the face mask on during the drive over, and it's not terribly far. To Deacon's credit, he plays my lord and savior Taylor Swift on the drive to wherever we're going, and I sing along with "Wildest Dreams," really getting into it, then ask Deacon to play it again.

He's amused, and he turns it on again as I dance exaggeratedly to it in the front seat with my "Fuck Off" mask on and the world cast in total darkness. I bob my head and use my water bottle as a microphone—yes, I'm overdue for a night of karaoke.

I feel the tires squeal over little pebbles, and I'm almost positive I know where we are now. Deacon kills the engine and comes around to open my door, helping me out of the truck. When he sweeps me up in his arms and carries me, a giggle escapes my lips. I can hear the gentle lapping of the water, so I suspect we're going to our favorite dock.

When he rips the mask off my face, I'm standing on the dock, pointing at Hans' boat.

"Surprise! The boat is ours tonight!" Deacon tells me, wrapping his arms around me from behind. "If you're wondering where I was yesterday, it was here, getting lessons on boating from Hans, filling the kitchen with your favorite drinks and snacks, and getting the place ready for us. Hans was so sweet, he cleaned the place for us before I arrived yesterday."

"Aww," is all I can manage, pressing my hand to my rapidly beating heart. Deacon slips back to the car to grab our bags and pillows, and I don't waste a second jumping from the dock to the boat and doing a celebratory dance when I don't stumble or trip. Grace isn't my middle name.

Deacon arrives and tosses me the items that I somehow catch without dropping them into the lake, and he tells me to go down to the cabin to get warm, but I'm not cold. I bring our things downstairs and see that there are candles every-where, card games on the little coffee table by the comfort-able two-person sofa, and the galley is piled high with snacks.

The place is spotless, and I run over to the bed, jump onto it, and flop onto my back. It's actually very comfortable, moderately soft without a single lump, and I release a happy sigh. I've never spent a night in a boat, barely ever been out in one, much less one that's going to be Deacon's in several months.

Then the boat starts moving, and I run over to the bridge to take a photo of my man at the controls of the boat. Deacon looks so sexy, all clean-shaven, smelling of my favorite Calvin Klein cologne and his woodsy aftershave. The scent had filled my nose throughout our entire drive here, intoxi-cating me and making me antsy to make love to him. I'm always ready for him, a stark contrast with my past.

We drop anchor when we get to the center of the lake, and then we meet up on the deck as the last beams of sunlight bow to the dark blues and purples of evening. Deacon lights candles that the light breeze tries to snuff out. The late autumn chill sneaks up my spine, so Deacon tightens the throw blanket around me and whispers, "Snug as a bug in a rug."

It's something my dad used to say to me. I'm not sure if I've ever told Deacon about it, but the sweetness of the phrase makes me misty-eyed. There's magic in the air, and the purple LED lights glow bright enough for us to see each other clearly The candlelight scatters shadows across Deacon's face as he smiles down at me, his arm coming around my shoulders to pull me closer.

"It's so peaceful here," I whisper. "Surrounded by the gentle waves, under this purple sky."

"Hold on," Deacon tells me. "There's so much more. It's just a waiting game."

I have no idea what he means, but I turn until I'm on my back with my head in his lap as I stare up at the sky. His fingertips dance across the exposed skin of my face and neck. He leans down to kiss my forehead, and tells me, "I love you so much, Aspyn Beckett. We were made for each other. You do know that, right?"

"I know." I nod in confirmation. "And I love you more than anything. You've been patient and loving for so long, and I can't wait for the rest of our lives."

Deacon and I lock eyes, and then he glances up and smiles. I follow suit, and when I look up, I'm dazzled by the stunning Northern Lights that streak and swirl across the sky. Closest to the water is a thick band of neon green, leading up to a brilliant fuchsia that seems to go on forever.

"Holy shit! It's—it's so close to my tattoo!" I realize as wonder consumes me. It's not my first viewing of the aurora borealis, but it's my first from the middle of a lake with the love of my life beside me.

But Deacon is no longer at my side when I glance back. I sit up, the blanket sliding down, and notice he's carefully pushed the table in the other direction, and now he's down on one knee at my feet.

He holds up an open box featuring the set of black diamonds I'd selected from his mother's rings, and he gives me a wide smile and says, "Beck, baby, I love you. I've loved you every minute for the last ten years, and I'll love you every minute until the day I die. I can't wait another second to beg you to be my wife. Be mine forever. Marry me, Aspyn Lane Beckett. Please?"

Tears stream down my face at his sincerity, the way his eyes stare at me like I'm the most spectacular thing on this lake under the Northern Lights. I drop to my knees, press my chest to Deacon's, and I manage a nod. "Yes, of course." I encircle my arms around his neck and melt my lips to his with all the love and affection in my heart, joy spreading through my veins as the Northern Lights twinkle their approval in the epic way only they can. When we stop kissing, we stand up, and Deacon slides both rings onto my left finger. They fit perfectly. The brilliant colors overhead hit the black diamonds and rubies on my finger, and they twinkle almost as bright as the stunning lights above us.

Deacon rocks me in his arms as I rest my chin on his shoulder and stare up, suddenly feeling a presence so strongly, I can't deny it. The hair on my arms stands on end, not in a scary way, but one that knows something I can't explain is happening.

I whisper, "I think your mom is looking down on us. I feel her here. If you have something to say, I think this is your moment."

Deacon looks thoughtful and finally looks up at the sky.

"Mom, if you're here, just know that everything worked out the way it was meant to. You were right all along, as always. I should have told you it was okay for you to go, Mom. Shouldn't have begged you to stay like that."

Tears drip down Deacon's face. "I wish I had made it easier on you. It's okay that you had to go, and I hope you're out of pain now. And I'll be better at looking in on Dad and my brothers, I promise. I should have told you *I got this* because I do. I love you, Mom. Thanks for stopping by."

Two shooting stars streak across the bright pink sky, and I wipe Deacon's tears before kissing every part of his face.

"She'll probably stop by at the wedding, too," I tell him before I kiss him deeply, and the night turns into one we celebrate until we fade off to sleep as the sun rises.

$\maltese$ 24 $\maltese$

ASPYN

It's only five days later when I wake up on a beautiful morning, the sun streaming in through the curtains, and catch a glimpse of Deacon staring at me. He's propped up on his elbow beside me in bed. I give him a smile, glance at my rings, and the reality hits me like a freight train, the same way it does every single day.

I'm going to be his wife!

"Good morning, dream girl," Deacon whispers, leaning over to give me my usual good morning kiss. Even when he wakes up early to go to the office, he never forgets my kiss. "So, I've been thinking..."

I giggle. "Uh oh." I wipe my eyes and yawn, barely out of my dreams yet.

"How would you like to get married today?" Deacon's gaze searches my face as my eyes widen. My mouth falls open in shock as I stammer, "What do you mean, get married today? It's like a regular Friday, a week before Thanksgiving, and we haven't planned anything! Not to mention the fact we've barely shared with anyone that we're engaged because we want to do it at Thanksgiving!"

Deacon chuckles with a twinkle in his eye. "Hence my suggestion. The justice of the peace at City Hall has a two o'clock slot free today, and I don't want to wait another minute to make you my wife. We don't have to tell anyone if you don't want to, but I think we should call Steele, ask him to be our witness, and pledge our undying love to one another before the day is over. It just feels like today is the day. I woke up with a sense of urgency I can't explain. Maybe it's crazy, Beck, but I love you so fucking much, I can't handle a long engagement. I need you to be mine forever, starting now."

I gulp. "It's a big ask at 6 a.m. on a Friday." I sit up and lean against the tufted headboard. I want our friends and family to share in our special day, but maybe what they don't know won't hurt them. We could still have a wedding, and getting married to Deacon by the day's end? The more I think about it, the better the idea sounds. After all, I'm ready to be Deacon's wife, and to call him my husband. We could play it close to the vest until the right time.

"You've convinced me, Deac. Let's do it." I make the decision, grab his hand, and squeeze it tight. "I love you, and if this is how you want to do it, I'm game!"

"Oh, thank god. Thank you, Beck. I'm so happy!" Deacon claps his hands excitedly. "You're going to be my wife by 2:15!"

Holy shit. What will I wear?

"Wait, I have a cream-colored dress somewhere," I realize, kissing Deacon softly before I practically run to my closet to peruse my dresses, finally finding it. A tea-length, mid-weight, lace dress that hugs my curves perfectly, with puffy iridescent sleeves that are on trend for the fall. I rummage through my drawers and pull out a light blue lace bra with matching panties. "And I've got something blue."

He materializes behind me in the large, fancy closet. "Yes, you do. And something borrowed." Deacon holds out an expensive pearl necklace that had been his mother's.

"Oh, classy. That's going to be perfect!" I grin, taking the necklace into my hand and staring down at it. "Plus, I have blue shoes!" I rummage to grab the suede heels that I haven't had a worthy occasion for yet. They're fancy and smush my baby toe, but they're worth it.

After Deacon makes me a big breakfast, I use a wave crimper to turn my pink hair into beachy waves, and I step into the dress just as a knock comes at the bathroom door.

"Come in!" I yank the side zipper shut.

Steele appears, and he stands there with his mouth open for a few seconds before he manages an awed, "Wow."

I giggle. "Thanks, dude."

"I mean it. Really, really...wow. You look, well...Deacon's a damn lucky man!" Steele shakes his head. "You look lovely."

I blush. "You should see my shoes. They make my calves look hot. Here, stand there a second." I disappear back into my closet, slip on the expensive heels, and add a cream-colored faux fur cropped vest with leather fringe to give a Boho look. I peer into the mirror, loving the classy lace and leather look, and I walk back to the bathroom and give Steele a little twirl.

"You're just missing one thing. I set it on the bed. One sec." He reappears with a dainty white and blue flower crown.

I take the circle of flowers in my hands and try not to get teary as I carefully place it on my head and adjust it, so it fits just right. I add a few bobby pins to keep it in place and then apply a final coat of lipstick to my quivering lips. I press them together and sigh, unable to believe today is the day I become Deacon Ambrose's wife.

"It's perfect," Steele announces. "I'm so glad Deacon finally gets to be your husband. I won't lie and say I don't wish Mom were here to see it, because she would be so happy for you, but I'm glad you let me in on your little secret. How are you going to keep this one hidden?"

I snort. "Well, I'll do the best I can, just until we can have a proper ceremony. I'll start planning right away, aiming for spring. Where's Deacon? Is he ready?" My heart flutters with excitement, and I rub my hands together to create friction. It's a chilly day, and snow is expected later.

"Pacing like a crazy person waiting for you. He sent me here to check on you. You good walking in those heels?" Steele peers at me with concern. I laugh.

"I'm a woman. I was born with the ability to strut around in sky-high heels."

We share a grin, but he takes my elbow and leads me out to the living room. Deacon is pacing but stops the second he sees me coming down the stairs. He looks the most handsome I've ever seen him, navy pin-striped suit hugging his sculpted chest, his bright blue eyes in awe as he focuses on me.

I step forward, set my hands on his chest, and then kiss him deeply, thankful for my Color Stay lipstick.

"You clean up nice, love," I whisper against his lips.

"And you look like you stepped out of my wildest dreams." Deacon slants his lips over mine, plundering my mouth with his tongue as I wrap him tighter in the circle of my arms. When we finally part, he asks me to wait a second, and then he goes into the bedroom and returns with three aquamarine bangle bracelets. "I thought these would look nice with the blue shoes."

"Great taste. Obviously." I motion at myself and roll my eyes before I slide the jeweled bangles onto my right wrist and then move my hand until they clang out a rhythm. I grab my blue leather bag, shaped like a rose, with a long silver chain, and place my phone, wallet, and lipstick inside.

"Well, shall we get married or what?" I walk to the door. Deacon runs to keep up with me and helps me up into his truck. Steele jumps in the backseat, and we drive ten minutes to City Hall.

Everything happens fast. The justice of the peace allows us to hook my phone up to a speaker, so I walk down the aisle to the perfectly timed chorus of one of my favorite songs. Deacon and I had agreed to take traditional vows, so I walk to him, stand beneath a wooden arch, and slide my hands into his.

Our eyes are transfixed on one another's, and I can't believe how lucky I am, how everything lined up perfectly in my past to get us here to this day. To this moment. I repeat the vows with my whole heart.

I'm marrying my best friend. My forever.

Not everyone gets to do that. Not everyone gets the fairytale, but me? I do. We do.

"As long as we both shall live," I hear myself say through tears, in a bit of a haze. The ceremony is short, and we'd cut right to the good stuff while Steele recorded us from several feet away.

"Well, then, by the power vested in me by the state of Colorado, I now pronounce you married. You may kiss your bride, Mr. Ambrose," the justice of the peace tells Deacon.

He breaks into a face-splitting grin, grabs me, dips me, and brings me back up to his waiting mouth. I melt into his arms, joy and peace washing over me as we kiss deeply, a few too many seconds for the occasion.

"I love you, wife," Deacon tells me tearfully, picking me right up off my heels and twirling me around several times with a disbelieving laugh.

"I love you, too. Husband." I can't believe how perfect it sounds rolling off my lips. "But you've gotta put me down, you're making me dizzy!"

We both giggle as I try to slide my feet into my heels. Then, we embrace again, kissing until the older man beside us clears his throat and reminds us he has another wedding to conduct.

As we walk together out the front door of the building, holding hands, the skies open up and light snow swirls around us, but I hardly feel the cold.

We walk into the adjoining courtyard and pose for photos that Steele takes with his fancy camera. I feel lucky to have him with us today as our witness and photographer.

We again swear Steele to secrecy as we drive home, and Steele pecks me on the cheek, hugs his brother, and climbs into his SUV. Deacon must have been giving him a look that said, "Scram!" because as soon as Deacon shuts the front door, he unzips my dress and lets it pool at my feet.

"Hot tub?" Deacon holds out his hand for me to take. I love to sit in the hot tub while it snows, and he knows it. I agree. I yank down my blue thong. But he doesn't let me get far before he kneels between my legs and plunges his tongue into my center. He stops just short of letting me come, picks me up, and then sets me gently down in the hot, bubbly water as he turns on a playlist that I'd watched him make this morning. Bruce Springsteen's "Secret Garden" comes on. It's our playlist, full of songs meaningful to both of us, ones that make us think of each other. I'd given him several titles when he'd quizzed me over coffee.

A few minutes later, I straddle Deacon and ask, "Ready to consummate this marriage, my love?"

I don't get a chance to answer. Deacon silently thrusts up to join us together. I moan and move against him, leaning down to kiss him between groans and grunts. Deacon's hands on my ass guide my movements, and he gives me long, slow strokes in and out that leave me dying for him. My body is superheated as he drives me over the edge, feeling like a pool of mush as he comes hard and deep, crying my name and gasping out, "Wife!"

After a few quiet moments, he withdraws, and I jump out of the hot tub to clean up in the bathroom.

"Don't even think I'm done with you yet, baby," Deacon warns me. "I want to fuck you into oblivion."

My stomach flutters with anticipation. *Hell yes.*

"Let's do that," I wink. I glance down and see the mark he's left on my left breast. "Look at you, trying to mark me or something. You already have a wedding ring on my finger to do that, you goof."

A smile spreads to Deacon's face as he shrugs. "Accidental but enjoyable. Bring those breasts back here."

I giggle while I oblige, jumping back into the hot tub and letting Deacon shower my nipples with affection. After about twenty minutes of steamy petting, we're both too warm to stay another minute. He chases me into the bedroom, where he lays me down and makes love to me gently and tenderly, whispering words of love as he brings me to orgasm after orgasm.

My husband, my husband, my husband echoes in my head as I convulse on top of him, drawing out my last orgasm as long as possible.

"Don't stop," I plead, throwing my head back with a moan.

"Never," Deacon swears, continuing to thrust as I gush around him. "God, you're so beautiful. And mine!"

"All yours!" I brace my hands on his thighs, changing the angle until it's perfect. I never want it to end, but all good things do, and eventually, we wind up sprawled out across the bed, our limbs intertwined.

"This is everything I've ever wanted," Deacon tells me, kissing me until I push him away to catch my breath. "I'll try to make you as happy as possible every day of the rest of our lives, Beck. I mean it. Your happiness is all I want."

Deacon traces his fingers across my face and presses his finger into my chin dimple as I smile. "I think it's the time of year for joy."

25

DEACON

I underestimated how difficult it would be not to shout from the rooftops, "Beck married me!" Some of Beck's friends are still warning her how she should take "time to heal," which throws her off. She tells me Sean rarely crosses her mind anymore, but he still drifts into mine, even after a lifetime of friendship.

We're in the kitchen making breakfast when Beck tells me, "I think Tara knows. Or she thinks she knows. Tells me she knows I have a secret, and she's gonna get it out of me."

I laugh. "Oh, no. She's persistent, too. How about your parents? I'm having a rough time not telling Dad!"

"Well, at least we told him at Thanksgiving that we were engaged. My parents were very happy to hear about our engagement when I told them last week, as you know. They keep calling, asking us to fly out to Japan for Christmas, but I just want to enjoy a quiet holiday. I finally told them no last night," Beck tells me as she flips pancakes.

"We can visit another time. I hear it's beautiful there! I finally put in our RSVP to the Wright family Christmas party.

You're sure you're ready to face that prick? Sean is going to be there, I'm sure."

"He's in the past, where he belongs. I think I can stand being in his presence once a year. Besides, you'll be with me, and you're all I need." Beck wraps her arms around me tightly and squeezes as I move the bacon around in the pan. "Oh, I did hear from Tara that his girlfriend, Quinn, is coming. It's weird to put a name to Nurse Q. It seems less sexy than I imagined."

I chuckle at the thought.

"Anyway, I guess she's an earthy type, really into the outdoors. Sounds like he found my replacement fast, huh?" Beck grins. "I hope she realizes Sean wouldn't be caught dead in the woods, and he'd feed her to a bear to spare himself!"

Beck lets me go and plates some pancakes.

"Well, hey, I'm glad that talking about him doesn't upset you so much anymore. I don't disagree with you about the bear. Sometimes I think of Sean, but I said everything I needed to say, and until he can figure out how to be a better person, I'm okay with the radio silence," I tell Beck.

"You deserve a better friend than Sean. I'm glad the guys didn't choose sides, though I think they would have taken yours," Beck replies.

So far, even Sean's cousin Jett had continued talking to me and inviting me to hang out regularly. Everyone seemed to understand who the guilty party was, and they also seemed happy for us about our engagement, although there were whispers of "too soon." But Beck and I, we're on our own timeline, and none of those whispers matter.

When Beck told Marissa about our engagement, she taunted her, saying she "knew it all along" that I was always a better fit for Beck than Sean. I appreciate that the girls are all on our side and cheering on our relationship. They can see that Beck is truly happy now.

"What are you thinking about?" I ask her as we sit down at the kitchen table with our breakfast spread and a carafe of coffee.

"How excited I am about our May wedding plans! I'm glad we booked the venue I wanted. I'm going to love the incredible mountain view, even if we freeze our asses off outside." Beck grins widely.

I shrug. "People can wear coats if it's chilly. Who knows? With climate change, maybe it'll be a hot day. We'll keep the ceremony quick, and head inside the resort afterwards. I'm glad we agreed to keep things small, just the people we truly love. Are you sure we should invite Sean's parents?"

Beck guffaws as she chews a huge bite of pancake. "Come on, babe. They've been like second parents to both of us for a long time. Cecile wants to throw us an engagement party, and if I say no, she'll insist on hosting the bridal shower. She loves us."

Beck has a point. She's usually right. I've stopped fighting that. I think about the ring on her finger and what it means for the rest of my life. How lucky I am to call this woman mine. Waiting over a decade had been the right thing to do, no matter how many times people told me to get over it and move on with my life.

The only life I want is one with Aspyn Beckett—and it's the life I have.

Ten years of best-friendship had been enough to feel absolute certainty that Beck is the right one, for now and forever. I never want to look at another woman. She's captured my heart so fully, it will always be in her hands. Marrying her was the easiest decision of my whole life.

The fact that she's now Aspyn Beckett Ambrose makes me the happiest man in the entire world. Though, she's always been Beck to me and always will be.

"My turn to ask what you're thinking." Beck sips her coffee and looks over at me expectantly.

"How fucking delighted I am that you took my last name." I give her a look of disbelief and shake my head. "And how did I get so lucky?"

"Mm, you think you're lucky now. Wait until the food settles, and you may find yourself even luckier."

Like I said. Luckiest guy ever, maybe in the entire universe. I glance over into her hazel eyes that shine mischievously and green, and Beck's beauty steals my breath. *So. Lucky.*

Suddenly, Beck looks morose, and I demand, "What's wrong?"

"It's just, I'm scheduled for a birth control shot Monday since the pills are making me so crazy. And I don't want to do it, Deac." Tears well up in her pretty eyes, and she swipes them away. I lean closer and take her face in my hands.

"Why is that, love?" I need to hear it out loud.

"I've always wanted a big family like the one you have. Being the only child wasn't my favorite experience, and I'm already almost thirty. If we don't start soon..." Beck trails off and then adds, "I want to start soon. Though, we haven't had much of a honeymoon period, but who knows how long it will take for me to get pregnant?"

I long to put my hand over her mouth, but I restrain myself. She's about to speak, but I interrupt and give her my most dazzling smile. "Then, let's have babies, Beck."

She jumps out of her chair and squeals. "Are you sure? I don't want to rush you, and I know that—"

More firmly, I tell her, "Let's start in half an hour when the food settles."

Beck throws herself into my arms, nearly knocking me off my chair. I stand up, squeeze her tight, and twirl her around like I did the day we were married. By the time I put her down, she's crying happy tears and bobbing her head happily.

"I've never wanted anything more than to have a family with you, my love. You're the light of my life, and our children will be so lucky to have you as a mother. You love fiercely, have so much compassion, and you're one of the smartest women I've ever met. Loyal to a fault. Courageous. You'll raise our children to be kind, loving people who make the world a better place. I'm ready to do this with you. Today. Tomorrow. Whenever." It's as easy as that.

Beck sobs lightly, and I cover her mouth with mine. We leave the food on the table as I lead her up the stairs and back to our bed, where I show her just how eager I am to give her the baby she longs for.

❦ 26 ❦

ASPYN

The day of the Wright family Christmas party arrives, and I spend the morning and afternoon getting ready and giving myself the necessary pep talks. At Deacon's urging, I had selected an incredible new dress that started with black satin at the top and then transitioned from black satin into a maroon-to-pruple ombre, with a wide, full skirt covered in beading. The deep V of the neckline stretches down past my sternum, necessitating that I tape my breasts in place. I know, looking in the mirror, I've never owned a more beautiful gown, and I feel so pretty in it. Deacon had bought it for me as if it were no big deal, just tossing his debit card down and announcing, "We'll take it!"

Now I'm fussing with my hair, curling it perfectly. It's gotten long, and Deacon loves it this way. More to pull, I guess. God knows we've been spending a lot of time in bed lately, giving each other endless pleasure in our quest to get pregnant. We're twenty minutes late to the party because Deacon insisted on bending me over the couch and taking me hard while I held the dress up.

When we ring the doorbell, Sean's father, Matthew, opens it, and his mother Cecile walks over to welcome us in.

"Thank you so much for the invitation," I tell Cecile.

She pulls me into her arms and says, "I miss you!" in my ear. "And my darling, you have never looked more beautiful. You are absolutely glowing. And you, Deacon." She looks him up and down and smiles. "You're looking dapper as ever in that tux. Happiness suits you well."

"I couldn't agree more." Matt claps Deacon on the shoulder. "To know you two are so happy together is a real relief for us. We love you like you're our own children and are so glad that you both came tonight. Sean has been ordered to be on his best behavior."

I tear up a little at Matt's sweet words, and I give him a big hug. "Thanks. Life's too short for unhappiness. I'm glad everything turned out so well in the end. The universe always provides, right?"

"It does," Matt agrees. "Oh! The deviled egg tray is making its rounds. Go grab yourself a plate. I know they're your favorite."

I giggle and wave, then practically sprint off to the plates. I get in prime position to scoop several eggs unabashedly. Deacon makes his way over with a flute of champagne for me. I'd taken a test this morning and gotten a negative, so I throw back the deviled eggs and then gulp the sweet bubbles without guilt.

"In here!" Tara calls. I glance around and spot her sitting with Cody and our friends in the adjoining game room, gathered around the pool table. Usually, Matt and Cecile like to keep it closed during parties, but nobody gives a shit today, so we make our way in, scanning the room as I step toward our friends. Deacon has my hand tightly clasped in his.

"He's not in here. Take a breath," Deacon whispers. "And you can stop squeezing my hand to death."

I release my grip on his hand and embrace Tara, Cody, Wendy, Jett, and then Marissa.

"Hey, you're all looking gorgeous! Who's gonna get me something stronger than champagne?" I hold up my empty flute and pout.

"I got it," Jett tells me, heading over to the bar in the corner to fix me a glass of whiskey and Coke. When I take it and throw a few sips back, I ask, "Has anyone seen Sean?"

"He and Quinn are arguing loudly in the car." Marissa rolls her eyes as Bear walks into the room and apologizes for being late. "And you should know before they come in here, she's *huge*. And also, nowhere near as pretty as you are, Aspyn. Cute at best. By the way, holy shit, girl, you look hot tonight! That dress fits you like a second skin." Marissa whistles and catcalls me.

I take the compliment gracefully and finish my whiskey and hand the glass back to Jett for a refill. He snorts as if he knows exactly why I'm drinking so fast and returns promptly with another glass.

"Wowza," Tara agrees as I do a little shimmy and grin.

"Thanks, Marissa, Tara. And we don't have to shit-talk her. I'm happier now with Deacon than I ever was with Sean. She can have him. At least I don't have to spend my life with that asshole. Sorry, Tara."

"No sorry needed. I'm inclined to agree." Tara sips her red wine. "Quinn is fairly nice, but you're the only one I've ever wanted for a sister-in-law."

"Well, unfortunately for Quinn, that's a role she'll likely be playing. But you'll always be my friend." I encircle my arm around her shoulders and squeeze. "I love you."

Tara hugs me back and sighs. "I love you, too. Oh, there's Quinn's voice. It's annoying."

"I finalized the flowers for the wedding," I tell the girls as the guys step to the side to talk about cars. "I'm going to stick mostly with wildflowers, and we'll do flower halos for all the bridesmaids. I won't be wearing a veil or be given away or anything like that."

"The veil is when you feel bridal, not like a little kid dressing up in her mother's wedding dress. I can't explain it, but it's a real phenomenon. Just think about it, okay?" Tara argues with me.

"I want to wear my hair in a half-updo with the flowers braided in. I found a great photo—" I reach for my phone to find the hairstyle website when Sean's voice rings out.

"Ridiculous. You've managed to ensnare Deacon, but he will never marry you. He'll realize before this sham of a wedding happens that you're not right for him. You're the girl men date, not the one they marry."

I whip around and face Sean, an acrid taste in my mouth as he stands there with an expression of distaste on his face and his eyebrows raised high. Suddenly, Deacon materializes and shoves Sean, hard.

"Fuck you, Sean Wright, and don't you ever, ever talk about my wife like that again!" Deacon shoves him one more time for good measure. Sean almost loses his balance as his eyes bug out and the creases in his forehead pop along with that blue vein in the center of it.

"Wife? You're about five months too early. You still have time to get out of this!"

Deacon grabs my wedding band from his suit pocket and shoves it onto my hand, holding it up in the air right by Sean's face.

"We got married, asshole, and this woman is the best thing that has ever happened to me. You may have used, abused, and cheated on her with your new baby mama, but she's safe with me. I've got her forever." Deacon's red in the face by the time he finishes.

A hush falls over the room. That's when I notice a tall,

redheaded girl, visibly pregnant, standing outside the entrance to the room, her eyes wide with shock. She presses a hand to her open mouth, turns, and runs.

I don't know why I do it, but I chase her in my heavy dress and finally catch up to her near Sean's Range Rover as she leans against it, gasping.

"God, you're fast," I tell her as I hold up my hand and reassure her everything is okay. "I'm not here to make drama. I can see you're upset, so I...ran after you."

Maybe it's because I was her, and I wouldn't wish that fate on my worst enemy.

The short-haired girl begins to sob, and I find my heart unexpectedly aching for her over the man who had charmed her, and—for a long time—had both charmed and deceived me.

"I had no idea he was with you. How long were you together?" She looks horrified and red in the face. As she cries, she grows even redder and blotchier, sniffling loudly.

I try not to roll my eyes at how predictable this situation is. Sean is an excellent liar, and I can tell Quinn's telling the truth based on her reaction.

"Almost a decade. I'm sure you didn't know about me, mostly because Sean is a great liar. He had me thinking he was a decent guy for over nine years, all the while he gaslit me, making me think I was crazy, like I had to change every-thing about myself to win his approval. Does that sound familiar?"

Quinn wipes her face and nods. "So far, it's just little things. He hates that I eat pork."

I roll my eyes and nod. "Girl, I know. He's barely let me eat a piece of bacon in a decade. The little things grow into big things eventually, until you don't recognize yourself anymore. And he's incredibly controlling."

Quinn bites her lip. "He's already got the baby named, and

I hate the ones he's picked out. Sean's acting like it's his choice."

"Quinn, it's not you. It's him. This is just who he is. He's only happy when he's in control and controlling you entirely, if you do exactly what he wants you to do. Nobody can keep that up forever. You lose yourself, and that's never worth it. Look. I know he's charming, and I don't blame you for being charmed, but I want you to think about your baby and open your eyes before it's too late. Listen to the way he talks to you, pay attention to how he treats you. You've got to have an inkling that something about him isn't right. He cheated on me with you, and he'll cheat on you too."

Quinn sniffles, shaking her head. "I-I thought I was crazy! Like, he was so charming, so good for me before I got pregnant, and now he's like..." Quinn gasps for breath, wiping her cheeks. "Never happy! Nothing I do is good enough for him. He comes with me to the doctor's appointments and smiles, but there's like, nothing happy behind his eyes. I don't even know if he truly wants this baby."

Quinn sniffles and wipes her nose with the back of her hand. Then she stands up straight and widens her eyes. "I shouldn't be telling you this. I don't even know your name!"

I hold out my hand. "I'm Aspyn Beckett Ambrose. I'm sorry we're meeting this way."

She shakes my hand, albeit reluctantly.

"I didn't know, I promise. I have no idea what to say other than I'm so, so sorry. Ugh, I should've seen the signs, especially when he never wanted to take me home. There were all sorts of red flags, but I just ignored them. Now that the baby is almost here, I don't know what I'm supposed to do." I see the fear in her brown eyes and soften my expression.

"It's not your fault, Quinn. Like I said, he's an expert liar, and he fooled me for a long time. I'm far better off now without him, but I don't want his next victim to be you."

Quinn sighs. "I didn't move in with him, but I'm supposed to next week. The baby is due in early January, and I thought it would be good if he moved in to help take care of me after—"

I interrupt. "He won't. He'll find any excuse or say he's on call, and he'll leave you to do all the work. Do you have family? A support system?"

"I have two sisters in the area. My mother lives an hour away. She wants to come stay for a while after Vincent is born, but Sean is really against it."

I sigh loudly. "Listen, that's just what he does. It's there in the narcissistic abuse handbook, Quinn. He tries to separate you from your support system, so you totally rely on him. He'll make snide comments about them and point out their faults. He's not a nice guy. Sean is good at first, and he does well in a crowd or at a party like this one, but in the moments when you really need him, he won't rise to the occasion."

Watching Quinn's face, I see my comments hit her hard. Probably because she has already observed some of that behavior and has been reluctant to acknowledge it, as she wants Sean to be a good guy. She still has hope.

"He says nasty things about my mother and sister. They've been perfectly nice to him. What a dick." Quinn's voice spews venom now, and she asks, "What now? I can't pretend everything is fine."

"Why don't you go stay with your mom or sister? Let them take care of you." I feel genuine concern for the woman standing in front of me, hurting over the same man who hurt me so much in the past ten years. I want a different outcome for her than ten wasted years.

Quinn suddenly smiles. "My sister Jill has a whole guest house she's offered me. My lease is up January 1st, which is why I was going to move in with Sean. I felt uneasy about it, though, and you just confirmed all my worries."

I let out a sigh of relief. "Thank gods. I am sorry to be the one to dissolve your illusions. I had no intention of talking to you at all, much less telling you all these things you don't want to hear when you're so far along, but I'm glad you can see the red flags I couldn't at nineteen. And hey, Quinn? Thanks for hearing me out."

Quinn reaches up and puts her hand on my shoulder. "You're a kid at nineteen. All you see are green flags. Don't blame yourself. It wasn't your fault, no matter how much you blame yourself."

"Hey, let me see your phone," I tell her. When she hands it over, I input my contact info into it and hand it back to her. "There's my number. If you need to talk, well, I'm a therapist and would be happy to listen. I harbor no ill will toward you, and I truly wish you and Vincent the best."

I'm surprised when she throws her arms around me and hugs me close.

"What the fuck are you telling her?" Sean's voice demands from behind me as I let go of Quinn and step away.

"Scared I might be telling her the truth? I'm going to get back to the party and my husband. Thanks for cheating and setting me free, Sean. I gotta tell you, I've never been happier in my life, and you're the one who made it possible. Goodnight, Quinn."

I look at her over my shoulder, spotting fresh tears on her cheeks as Sean rants at her. Nausea invades my stomach as I realize what he's doing: love bombing her, saying all the right words, convincing her I'm crazy. He'll go into overdrive trying to keep her, to pacify her. He'll call me "histrionic," always one for big words.

Letting out a heavy sigh, I return to the party, finding Deacon amongst friends in the game room where I'd left him. When he spots me walking toward him, he holds out his arms and I fall into them.

"I told her the truth. Gave her my number. She already sees the red flags," I tell my husband.

"That was big of you, baby." Deacon kisses my temple.

"It was the right thing to do. He doesn't deserve her."

"That's why I love you. You know the right thing to do, and you do it without hesitating." Deacon kisses my forehead, and my friends swarm me with congratulations for our sneaky wedding ceremony.

Finally, I pull up a short video of the event, and everyone huddles around it, grinning as they watch us say traditional vows.

"You were stunning," Marissa whispers. My cheeks hurt as I smile, watching the wedding back for the very first time.

Steele walks up and agrees. "Yes, she was. I made her flower crown." He grins proudly and gives me a little hug.

Stefanie, Emmett's girlfriend, tells me, "I can't believe you got married without telling anyone!"

"Shh, it's getting to the good part," Tara hisses as we listen to Deacon and me say "I do," and then kiss like crazy. When it finally stops, a couple of my friends are in tears, and everyone hugs us both.

"Man, you guys went from zero to sixty, huh?" Cody asks as he holds Tara in his arms.

"When you know what you want forever, you go after it. You'd know a little about that," Deacon tells him. Cody holds out his hand, and they fist-bump. "And we hope you'll all still take part in our May wedding. We want to give our parents and families a nice ceremony. We just couldn't wait until May. You know how it is."

"Married, dearies?" Cecile asks from the doorway, having overheard the whole thing.

Matt is hot on her heels. "Who's married?"

Everyone laughs at Matt as Cecile walks over to Deacon,

embraces him, and tells him, "Lillian would be so happy for you and so proud of you. You finally got your girl."

"He did?" Matt asks, confused. "What did I miss?"

And as I look around the room full of my friends and my beloved husband, I take a mental snapshot of the moment and try to memorize it. I want to keep tonight with me forever.

I hold out my hand to Deacon. "Shall we dance, baby?"

"Always," Deacon agrees, walking me out to the living room where there's a makeshift dance floor.

The DJ quickly changes the song, and my face breaks out into a huge grin, because it's the same one we'd walked down the aisle to. Sometimes the universe really does get it right. Deacon pulls me into his arms, and we dance like nobody's watching, living our very own happily ever after.

Over the next month and a half, I struggle so much with morning sickness that I don't feel well enough to meet Quinn's little Vincent until the end of February. We received our pink plus sign in January, after my thirtieth birthday, and it was the best present Deacon and I could have ever hoped to receive.

Now, I'm driving my Durango to the other side of Colorado Springs, eager to meet my friend Quinn's little boy. We've talked on the phone and texted constantly since I helped her avoid the biggest mistake of her life, and she'd heeded my warnings and had broken up with Sean.

My jaw dropped when I walked through the door. Sean's on the couch holding little Vincent, who has nearly iridescent skin and adorable red curls on his head. His brown eyes are exactly the same as Quinn's.

"Hi," I whisper, kicking off my snow boots. "Where's Quinn? And what are you doing here?"

"She's changing. Spilled milk all over herself while pumping," Sean tells me. "And she finally let me come over, so I'm on my best behavior right now. Listen. I-I need to apologize to you for so much. I don't expect you to forgive me, I know I wouldn't forgive me. For everything. The cheating. It happened more than twice, starting three years into our relationship." Sean sighs.

My mouth gapes open as I blink rapidly, then I shake my head. "Are you kidding me? *Why* would you stay with me if you just wanted to be with other women?"

"I didn't not want to be with you. I wanted to have you and also have my fun elsewhere. I was selfish."

"Yes, you were." I don't yell at him the way I want to, because Vincent is calm, and there was a hush throughout the house.

"Listen, everything you told Quinn was warranted. You know she ended things with me, and I get it. I want to prove to her I can be a good dad, so she'll let me come back to visit more often. She's got full custody, and I'm here to prove that having me as a father is a better option than none at all." He sharply exhales.

Sean drops his eyes to the baby again and sighs. "He's the best baby in the world. So perfect. Look at these fingers."

I take Vincent's tiny hand in mine and admire his little fingernails as he clamps his hand down around two of my fingers. He's perfect, that's for sure.

"I'm in therapy." Sean looks up at me. "I know that's what I need to be worthy of Vincent. And I'm going to buy Quinn and Vinnie a house, without my name on it. I won't even have the keys."

"They deserve it," I whisper. "Babies deserve daddies, Sean, but only healthy ones, so keep your ass in therapy for good. Trust that Quinn knows best, follow her lead. If you truly want to be, I think you can learn how to be a good father. But it's going to require a selflessness you've never attempted before."

A shadow crosses his face. "You deserved so much from

me that I didn't give you. But Deacon did and he does, and I know it probably sounds weird coming from me, but I'm happy for you two."

I bite my lip because it sounds so foreign to my ears, and then I nod. "Thanks. Um, I'm pregnant, so I'll be having one of these adorable things before too long. We're over the moon about starting our family."

"Congratulations." Sean seems to mean it. "You always did want a big family."

I sigh. "Yeah. I guess you let me believe you did, too, huh? Anyway...Sean, I have forgiven you, you know. It took some time, but it's in the past. And, uh, if you want the blender or PlayStation back, I guess you could have them."

Sean shrugs. "It's just stuff, Asp. I replaced them. Was I mad at the time? Yep. You were smart to block my cell phone number." He gives a small smile. "I deserved it."

Quinn steps out of the shadows with a pleased look on her face, and I jump up to hug her tightly. "Hey, mama!"

"I should say the same to you," Quinn replies with an ear-to-ear grin. "I can't believe you haven't told me about your pregnancy yet! How's it going?"

"Nauseatingly?" I wince, and Quinn pulls me into the kitchen. She hands me a big package of candied ginger, and she tells me they're the best thing she'd found aside from cherry ginger ale to help with nausea.

"Thank you. It's so good to see you. I've been knocked on my ass since early January, and now I finally feel like I'm in the land of the living again. Just had a chance to meet your little bundle of joy, and he's so perfect!" I hug her again and whisper, "You're doing such a good job. He's a spitting image of you."

She fills a teakettle with water. "Thank you, my friend. Vincent is the best thing I have ever done, hands down. Hey,

I'll make you some peppermint tea. I swear by that too. How's Deacon? The most excited father-to-be on the planet?"

I giggle. "You could say that. He's already planning a gender-neutral nursery with tons of yellow and purple. I told him purple is for girls, but he reminds me it's my favorite color, so that's what the theme will be. He painted the walls a pale yellow and bought this huge sunset sticker-thing for the top corner of one of the walls. He knows how much I love sunsets. He pays attention."

Quinn gives me a little smile. "That guy loves the hell out of you. Smart man. You're the best, you know. Sorry to surprise you with Sean's presence."

I shrug my shoulders and smile. "It's okay. I'm not upset. We exchanged some words that needed to be said."

Quinn squeezes my shoulders. "Do you think I did the right thing letting Sean come here?"

I glance through the doorway in the kitchen and spot Sean changing Vincent's diaper on the far wall of the guest house.

"I hope so. He wants to be better. I wouldn't allow him to be your boyfriend because that's not what he's good at, but I'd consider letting him be a father to Vincent if he keeps up with therapy," I tell her honestly.

It takes everything in me to give him credit where it's due —he'd resisted therapy for a decade when he was with me, and now he has a beautiful son, and he's taken the initiative to get into counseling on his own.

Wonders never cease, and sometimes, people surprise you.

When the tea is ready, Quinn pours me a mug and hands me organic honey to sweeten it. We sit in the kitchen, warmed by the afternoon sunlight through her large windows, with a great view of Pike's Peak through the window above her sink.

"We're so lucky to live near such beauty," I smile as I glance out the window in awe. "I never tire of it."

"Neither do I. Honestly, I feel luckier every day now that I'm Vincent's mama. It's incredible how motherhood changes your life, redefines your definition of love, and everything you thought you knew about it. There's nothing quite like it."

"Speaking of love, did you hear that both Emmett and Stefanie, and Wendy and Jett got engaged? And I hear Bear found a ring. It's officially the wedding season!" My friends had reluctantly let Quinn into our friend group, and she'd become especially close with Tara.

"That's amazing! No, I had no idea. I've been in my own little world here, enjoying my three months off. The fact that I have to go back to work seems cruel and unusual. In Canada, they get an entire year of maternity leave, and even have paternity leave."

"We're the only developed nation that doesn't have federally mandated maternity leave," I tell her, remembering reading that in the newspaper recently. "It tells you what society values, and that's not the unpaid labor of motherhood."

"It's the most fulfilling labor you'll ever do. Yeah, I'm exhausted, but even at 2 a.m., I'm happy to see Vincent's sweet face and hear his little cry." Quinn smiles serenely, and I hope I have a similar experience. "And Aspyn? Thank you again for chasing me out to the Range Rover on Christmas. I don't think I ever thanked you properly for changing the course of my life for the better. You're selfless, you know that? That's going to make you an amazing mom."

I sniffle, holding back tears, and nod. "Thanks, girl. And thank you for listening and not assuming I was a vindictive ex-girlfriend blowing smoke up your ass. I'm so glad we're friends. Even if it's a trauma bond." I chuckle. "And I'm so glad you can walk me through my pregnancy and all the unknowns about delivery and postpartum."

"There's so much they don't tell you. But hey, let's not worry about that just now. Why don't we get lunch? I have Sean here on baby duty, so I can leave the house for the first time in what feels like...forever." Quinn sends me a bright smile as she stands and shoulders her purse.

I follow her through the living room as she tells Sean, "If you think this might be a test, that's because it is. Have any questions before we go?"

Sean shrugs. "I don't think so. I know where the refrigerated bottles are and how to warm them up. I do listen when you talk, you know."

"That's new," I retort, but I lighten it up with a grin. "And welcome."

"I'm trying," Sean says, and I know he is. I can tell.

Quinn kisses Vincent, and then we disappear into the cold, late February afternoon for a late brunch and some much-needed girl time. While eating tres leches cake after a Mexican brunch, I unblocked Sean's number from my phone. Not because I want to talk to him, but if he has an emergency with the baby, I don't want to be far away.

At the end of the afternoon, Quinn dismisses Sean. She tells him he passed her initial test but still has a long way to go. I'd never seen him look happier.

He waves to me from the doorway as Quinn practically closes the door in his face, and I hold back a laugh.

That's when Quinn lets me hold Vincent. In my arms, he makes cooing noises and looks up at me adorably; his thin little lips so perfectly kissable, I don't know how Quinn doesn't just peck them all day long. How does she get anything done?

As I stare down at him, I can't wait to have my baby in my arms. We've discussed names, and I think we've landed on

Emery Lillian for a girl and Sullivan Chase for a boy. While I'm hoping for a little Emery, a Sully would make me just as happy.

When I finally turn little Vincent back to his momma, I sigh and stand. "I should probably get home to my husband. He's texting impatiently. Acting like he thinks he can knock me up twice."

We both laugh. "Girl, go. Get some. One of us should."

With a hug, we part, and I drive back to the home that was once Deacon's and is now ours, and I ask him, "You coming?" as I shuck my clothes and walk up the stairs. He nearly trips over his own feet, leaving the couch and running up after me.

"How was your day?" Deacon calls from behind me.

"Vincent is perfect. Sean apologized. He's in therapy. I don't want to talk about Sean right now, though," I tell him as I throw the covers back and fold them along the bottom of the bed. They only get in the way.

"Legs open, baby," Deacon commands me, so I move the pillows and lie flat on my back, thighs parted obscenely as he covers my body with his. The sensation of his muscular, naked body pressing into mine is heady and thickens the air between us as I inhale shakily.

He traces his hands up my calves while kissing my stomach that's carrying our child. Eventually, his hands stop on my hips, and he presses his face to my stomach.

"I hope you're asleep for this," Deacon tells our baby. His slow, soft kisses drift around my body and then down between my legs, kissing my pussy fully, moving his lips around my mound and upper thighs, tickling and teasing. It's so much better when he makes me wait and beg.

Because I will beg.

After Deacon has kissed every inch of my thighs, hips, and belly, the tip of his tongue follows the path his lips had, and my legs start to close around his head as he licks down through my inner lips. I'm already ready to combust.

He pushes the top of my body back against the bed and whispers, "Be still, love. Let me taste you."

I cry out for him as he licks me again, warmth spreading through my body as I moan with pleasure and try to stay still for him.

"You're so delicious. Wonderful. Mine," Deacon says with a smile. "I could eat you like this every day and not get enough."

I feel my hips lift wantonly, and he grabs them and holds me to his mouth, pressing his tongue into me in earnest. I reach out but find nothing to hold on to except the bedsheets as he rocks his face against me, and my hips meet his movements.

"Yes!" I call out, spots appearing behind my tightly closed eyes. When Deacon begins to rub that sensitive spot at the apex of my thighs, I throw my head back and cry out. This torture is delicate but oh-so-intense, and I need more. More. I think I even whisper, "More."

His mouth moves up to gently lap at my throbbing bud, and I fill the quiet bedroom with loud, long moans while he continues to love me with his tongue. Deacon looks up at me, and the eye contact makes me shiver.

When he adds two fingers to the delicate torture, I nearly hit the ceiling, closing my eyes to the pleasure, the world just sunlight and black spots, my body no longer in my possession as I spiral into a merciless orgasm. I hear myself cry out for Deacon, beg for god, then scream out some broken "Yeses" as he never stops moving his tongue or fingers. I allow myself to be taken over by Deacon Ambrose, my husband and father of my child, welcoming him into my body over and over again. He controls the pace, and me, entirely.

"Good job, love. Come again," Deacon whispers before he

sucks me into his warm mouth and lashes me with his tongue.

I press my hands to my eyes, finding them wet with tears, and then I move to grip his golden hair and tug it. Deacon moans nearly as loudly as I do, loving all the pleasure he's giving me, and knowing his is next. The muscles in my whole body tighten and contort as my belly rises, and I shove closer to his mouth.

Eventually, I push Deacon onto his back and straddle his hips, reaching down to hold his length, and then I slide down onto it, taking him home into my body.

"You fit just right," I groan, still somehow surprised by how wonderful making love with Deacon feels.

"Like a puzzle piece," Deacon manages to say as he stills within me and lets me control the pace. He lifts to lick one of my nipples, surrounding it with his lips as he sucks. I lean closer to him, desperate for the attention. He hasn't been able to touch my breasts since I first got pregnant; they had been so sore! Maybe the worst of that is behind me now.

I begin to rock against Deacon, finding a motion that works perfectly. He lets me control the rhythm for a while, my head thrown back as I moan continuously, more blissed out with every in-and-out motion I create with my hips.

"I need you to stop being gentle and fuck me the way I need," I demand as Deacon's face contorts from holding back.

My words free him. He flips me over, settles between my thighs, and presses deep inside me as he kisses me, his open mouth taking, taking, taking. He sucks my lips, then my tongue, while holding himself up on his elbows to thrust rhythmically, hard, deep. I reach down, grab his ass, and pull him even tighter and more fully into me. He hits a spot within me that sends me reeling over the edge, as I shriek, "Oh my *god!*"

"Again?" Deacon asks as he meets my eyes, which are nearly crossing with pleasure.

I lift my hips and drive him back against that spot, and he lets me fuck him for a while, as I tell him, "Again! Make me come."

Deacon repeats the movement that made me go completely wild. Until now, I held on to a shred of composure. Now I cry out animalistically, grabbing his hair with one hand and his ass with the other as I encourage him to keep going. I let my hand run up and down his back, admiring his sculpted ass as he thrusts into oblivion and makes me lose all sense of self, time, and place.

I'm sure I'm in another universe when Deacon reaches down, strokes my clit, and drives into me harder than ever before. My broken scream echoes throughout the room, and I combust beneath Deacon as his hips shove unevenly, and he groans out, "Oh, Beck," and empties himself deep inside of me. I feel every quiver and contraction as he spurts into me, and I'm still desperate for more.

Deacon drives into me a few more times and sends me over the edge into another spine-tingling orgasm. He sucks my nipple into his mouth and bites down as I come, tugging my hair hard and prolonging the orgasm into something endless and intense.

"Oh! Oh! Jesus!" I thrash beneath him.

When I finally still, we lie entwined together, the sound of our heavy breathing filling up the quiet room as the afternoon turns into night. I lie on his chest, more satisfied than I can ever remember being, his ring on my finger and carrying our baby that I can't wait to welcome to earth.

"Wanna show you something," Deacon finally manages to say after I stop shaking. He pulls me to my feet, though my knees still shake, and he leads me down the hallway.

He's applied the sunset to the wall of the nursery, and I

notice the white, circular crib sitting in the center of the room beneath a mobile of rainbows. The sheets are white with tiny silver boats on them, and there's a little wooden boat on the table beside the rocker he'd already purchased for me and the baby. A cream-colored, nautical-themed lamp sits beside the boat, featuring little ropes for handles and anchors on the lampshade in purple.

"You like the décor?" Deacon asks me as I run my fingers over the anchors.

"I love it." My voice is thick with emotion. "Did you paint this lampshade, Deacon?"

"Yes, and Dad whittled the boat and painted it, too. See?"

I pick it up, admire the detailed little yacht, and finally read the tiny letters that say, 'Love in the Sun.'

I smile up at Deacon from the rocker and put my feet up as I sigh in contentment. "I can't wait for the spring. We'll fish off the side of the boat. Invite our friends. Throw a big wedding for everyone to enjoy, even if I will be out to here in May." I put my arms out in front of my belly to demonstrate how pregnant I'd be on our wedding day.

"And then in October, we'll welcome our little one to the world." Deacon looks so distinctly at peace as he stares around the nursery and smiles.

He sinks to his knees and rubs my feet on the rocking ottoman, releasing a long, slow breath. "It's a strange feeling, having everything you've always wanted. There's nothing more I could ever ask for. Every wish has been fulfilled."

Deacon fiddles with the ring on my finger. "I feel Mom here."

"Hopefully you didn't feel her presence a few minutes ago," I retort as Deacon looks up at the sunset on the wall.

He shakes his head. "No, but I think she's pleased with the name we came up with. And I suddenly feel very strongly that we're going to have a girl. Emery Lillian. She's smiling down on us, and I think she wants us to call our baby Lily."

I hum low in my throat. "Lily, huh? That's beautiful. I could be convinced."

Deacon draws me into his arms and nods against my hair. "And she likes your pink hair." His hands tangle in my wavy locks as he pulls back and grins at me. "You've always been such a fucking angel, my love. We should fit you for a halo."

"Lillian, respectfully, we love you, but you might want to tune out now," I whisper skyward, pulling Deacon in for a long, deep kiss.

I take off running to the bedroom, and Deacon chases me. The one thing I know for sure? He'll always catch me.

NEWSLETTER

Let's keep in touch! If you've enjoyed my book, please sign up for my newsletter. Also, please consider leaving a review on Amazon or Goodreads! Even a line or two would be very beneficial for an indie author like myself. Thank you!

https://www.melissasengerauthor.com/newsletter-sign-up

ACKNOWLEDGMENTS

There are so many people I'd like to acknowledge...

To my critique partner, A—you're so wonderful! I value your hard work, friendship, and honesty more than you know! Without you, I don't think I ever would have published.

Kaitlyn—thanks for all you do and for your friendship, too.

Thanks to Krys for answering so many questions for me on this journey—I appreciate you!

To my friends who have encouraged me and basically bullied me to get my work out there for people to read, although it continues to terrify me.

For my husband and my son, who patiently put up with me spacing out constantly, either writing books in my head, on paper, or on my laptop. Without your understanding and support, there's no way I'd be able to be an author. I love you both.

ABOUT THE AUTHOR

Melissa Senger is an emerging contemporary romance author, originally from the suburbs of Chicago. She currently resides outside of Houston, Texas, with her husband, her 11-year-old son, her mother, and her three sweet pit bulls. She loves reading, painting, music bingo, Taylor Swift, and bringing her literal dreams to life in her books. You can find her in the kitchen with music blasting, sipping espresso with a baby name book in hand, ranting to her husband and mother about her latest plot hole and wondering why characters can't just name themselves.

If you've enjoyed this book, please consider leaving a review on Amazon or Goodreads. Even a line or two means so very much to the author as an indie writer with a small budget starting out.

Connect with the author on her socials! She'll always try to write back to you if you message, and she will follow you back.

Keep an eye out for the author's newest book, For Me, It's You, coming late fall 2025!